Magickal Morose

Emily Carol

For Steve and Midnight

The majority of my melancholy was dark, violent, and menacingly vivid. I wrote disturbing, disgusting, and insensitive reflections about both myself and the people around me. Mental illness is cruel and immersive: it blinds and lies.

Self injury is not healthy; it captures and controls.

Food is not an enemy; it is nourishing and necessary.

Fat is not bad; fat is not ugly. Bodies vary immensely, and there is beauty and joy in all sizes.

I apologize for my ignorance, for my hate, for my poison, and for my sorrow. We are not alone in our experiences, and all of our lives are singular, special. May we all find peace!

- Emily Carol Ruth Liles

Mental Health Resources:

Suicide and Crisis Lifeline: 988 or 1-800-273-TALK [8255]

National Hopeline Network: 1-800-784-2433 (1-800-SUICIDE)

Trevor HelpLine / Suicide Prevention for LGBTQ+ Teens:
1-866-488-7386

Crisis Text Line:Text HOME to 741741

Gay & Lesbian National Hotline: 1-888-THE-GLNH
(1-888-843-4564)

Teenline: 310-855-4673 or text TEEN to 839863 (teens helping teens)

National Eating Disorder Association (NEDA) HelpLine:
1-800-931-2237 or text NEDA to 741741

National Association of Anorexia Nervosa and Associated Disorders(ANAD): 630-577-1330

National Council on Alcoholism and Drug Dependence (NCADD):
1-800-622-2255

Partnership for Drug-Free Kids: 1-855-DRUGFREE or text your message to 55753

Substance Abuse and Mental Health Services Administration (SAMHSA): 1-800-662-4357

Journal Excerpts and Personal Essays.................1

Journal Excerpts and Personal Essays

There once was a strange [one] named Em
Who had not a clue how to swim
[They] fell in a well
Sank straight down to Hell
And never was heard from again
                    -Limerick by Emily Carol (age 11)

Emily Carol

I've been around a lot longer than I've been alive: an entity manifested alongside an early printing press, a ghost disguised as a breeze, a mentally ill whimsy goth with an eternal and unnerving need to spill into the world around me.

I returned to art. I returned to the cello. I always wanted to be a writer, so I figured it was time to return to my words as well.

I intended to create some sort of project from my psychiatric misfortune; however, I consistently put it off. I took the time to make short journal entries stating how I needed to write more— to get out the thoughts. *Maybe your mind will organize itself as you go through your memories.* I started with such enthusiasm and then lost motivation. I am not some extraordinary case, but, perhaps, that may be an even better reason to share about my mental health: I am not abnormal in my experiences, and so I hope that my seemingly ordinary case (as psychiatric adventures go) can resonate with others and help them feel less lost, embarrassed, or confused. Maybe by sharing the cruel parts of *myself*, someone won't feel so terrible about *themself*. Terrible like I sometimes do. The longer I take to address and reflect upon my mental health journey (that blasted Meddlesome Melancholy), the more terrible I feel about the thoughts I had and the behaviors I exhibited.

Some of my self-hatred has not diminished with time, but I can soften it and use it instead as a guide to understand why I did the things that I did: approach myself with compassion, reflect, and create something that evokes a better understanding of myself. There is a lot of shame involved in my journey. I did, thought, and said terrible, disturbing things. What I do know, now, is that I am a good person who accepts my darkness as a significant and important part of myself.

When I was in lower elementary school, I was introverted and definitely enjoyed my alone time (be it playing by myself entirely or engaging in quiet, parallel play), but I was not shy. I wanted to befriend everyone, and I didn't have too many significant complications with other children. However, time passed and my peers aged into the mindset that anything different than "normal" was bad. I was born already full of love and joy, inquisitiveness and creativity. I was enamored with the darkness as well: a gothic spirit from before birth, it seems. I found beauty in the shadows that so many people too often disregarded or refused to acknowledge: gore, terror, adorably terrifying creatures– the odd things that are in no way wrong to appreciate and love.

My first recollection of an auditory hallucination happened when I was four or five. When I experienced anxiety, I heard classical music (more specifically, a version of Pachelbel's Canon in D that my mom often played in the car). If not music, then I heard what sounded like marching with an occasional buzzing of wings, which, in my reality, belonged to an army of bug-like warriors who marched back and forth outside my window to protect me. I did not think anything about those experiences. I did not speak about them. They were soothing and I didn't have any reason, at that age, to believe they were unusual. I also did not realize that it was anxiety that I felt, as I had not yet learned the concept of anxiety or how to identify it in myself.

(In fact, many of my observations will be addressed and reflected upon from the perspective of where I am at today, and, ultimately, from the understanding I currently have of my disorders. This goes for my gender and sexuality as well– of course I did not know the terminology at the time, although I would have enjoyed having had that language to better express myself.)

I've been a maladaptive daydreamer since early childhood. A part of myself was always off in another world, and the grounding rituals I have since developed do not pull me out of that state, but rather help me to maintain an understanding of how to properly function based on my surroundings. I've also dissociated regularly since early childhood. However, like with my auditory hallucinations, my daydreams and dissociations were comforting and I am sometimes still pretty pleased with my ability to self-soothe, even if it may not always be the most healthy strategy.

I liked oddball creatures, violence, death, and sorrow, and I liked to approach them with soft, curious enthusiasm. I've always had a strong relationship with death; I learned how to better recognize death and how to comfort and guide others both to and from it. I know that many individuals in alternative subcultures understand the macabre; they know that, although something may be different, it is not inherently dangerous (after all, there is danger everywhere; to like what is spooky and dark won't turn me into some fire breathing demon– although I think I'd quite enjoy that and would excel in it). I was more threatened with death and violence

3

in Bible school from normal, "good Christian" adults– those "average joes" who were so biased, bigoted, and shallow from narrowed, neurotypical perspectives that found faults in anyone who didn't follow one specific path. When you're a young, aspiring "baby bat", it is inevitable to be accused of being some type of "evil".

Luckily, my mom was and is kind, and, despite her strict religious, emotionally abusive upbringing, she had the insight to purposely raise my siblings and me to be unapologetically true to ourselves. She never pointed out the differences that I should look for in others or in myself– I genuinely thought of people as just "people" upon meeting them, regardless of skin color, gender, spirituality, interests, etc... If I didn't get along with someone, then I'd just think, "oh well!" Differences were never as big a deal to me as they seemed to be for so many others. I am lucky. I had warmth and a freedom to be creative in my development of myself.

With that creativity, I learned to present myself on the outside how I felt on the inside. I thought it was wonderful, but I was bullied for it. Bigotry is so easily and so vehemently instilled into us. Both adults and kids nitpicked and ridiculed, mocked and degraded, but I was both fairly well behaved and a good student (albeit a strange one), so there wasn't too much more they could do other than say, "If you act normal, they won't pick on you" or "You're just doing it for attention anyway. You'll grow out of that." Well, to those who would say that: I'm still a witch, a goth, and, ultimately, a silly goose of a person (if that goose were haunted). And I still own and rock some of the clothes that I wore back then, so I, quite literally, haven't grown out of it.

On top of my budding mental health issues, I was also confused and frustrated with my gender: when I was a kid, I never felt like a girl. I also never felt like a boy. I didn't have words for how I felt. I didn't really identify with most human characters in books and shows. If there were any spunky ones who broke gender norms, then I definitely gravitated towards them (they were often queer-coded villains). I preferred films about animals (preferably the ones that were just basic and naked, not given clothes or breasts or long eyelashes, etc...). Fantasy creatures were the best, but, many times, they ended up being depicted as evil and were killed. I played with stuffed and plastic animal toys over dolls because they were more easily made gender-neutral. When auditioning for plays, playing "house", or acting out musicals with my sister, I was often the pet or the male character. They usually had more development, and the people I was playing with usually wanted to be the girl character; I didn't care either way, as long as I could play and not be a pretty princess: I *liked* pretty princesses, but I definitely didn't want to be one. I told my mom to refer to

4

drive-through toys by what they were, such as "Neopets" or "Star Wars", instead of "girl" or "boy" toys, and would get so frustrated by pointlessly gendered products and marketing.

I slept over at a boy's house when I was around ten or eleven, and I remember some of my classmates thinking it was weird for a girl to have a sleepover at a boy's house. Back then, my first thought was, "well, I'm not a girl." Now, my first thought is, "um...we were in fourth grade and watched movies and played Clue and then fell asleep. What in the hootin' holler were you thinking we kids were gonna do?" I felt alien, and I didn't have the terminology or characters to point to to say, "This! This is how I feel and what I am!" Now I'm better able to find characters to relate to, whether they're written as cis characters, queer characters, animals, creatures, robots, etc...I'll observe and gravitate towards personality traits, regardless of gender; however, I'm so, so delighted that LGBTQIA+ representation continues to grow. It's beautifully beneficial for children to experience queer representation: it can help them feel more validated, understood, and comfortable.

I'm only just now beginning to feel comfortable with my body. I know who I am, and am relieved. I only wish I knew earlier; I only ever knew what I wasn't. It's nice to both understand and feel like myself. When people say cruel and transphobic remarks or poke fun at the community, I file it away in my brain. I did it even before I knew exactly what they were doing. I remember, and I tell myself to be on guard when around them or people that remind me of them– a sad truth for too many.

I am lucky to be surrounded by loved ones who are open-minded and kind, and I have no qualms about whether or not bigots offend themselves with their own poisons; their hatred deserves discomfort. I am a trans-nonbinary bisexual whimsy goth witch with anxiety disorder, panic disorder, and borderline personality disorder, and, my good golly gosh, it is so great to have the terminology to better describe myself. It took a few decades to find those words, but they always were and continue to be my truth (and fuck those bullies who would preach to keep anyone from being able to use words to both describe and exist entirely as themselves). I am so exhausted by society's villainization of anything that doesn't conform to its narrow view of how other humans should be.

Anxiety around numbers and time was consistent throughout my early childhood, but my depression didn't manifest until I entered junior high. My anxiety worsened. I began to self harm around age twelve, although I do remember jumping off the side of a slide when I was in kindergarten– I'm unsure why; it may be that I was just seeing what would happen. I was young and curious. But a significant part of me felt like it

5

was from something dangerous in me that was trying to warn me of what was to come.

I did grow up with friends who genuinely cared about me; however, that did not negate the despair I felt consistently since I was a pre-teen. Mental illness does not care how much love you have. It does not care if you experienced trauma or if you had an uncomplicated childhood. There are no specific prerequisites to meet before you're bestowed with mental illness. I was a weird goth kid. I wasn't the best at expressing my emotions at that point; the "social butterfly" that my first grade teacher described me as was bullied out of me by upper elementary school. I withdrew. My anxiety worsened. I developed insomnia. I started to hate my body. I'd fixate on specific foods and put them into categories of "safe" or "chunky." The summer before my second year of high school, I stopped eating and spent most evenings running the track at a neighboring elementary school. My heart was stressed, and I had to wear a heart monitor for a few weeks. I never mentioned my diet, or rather, lack of diet, to the doctors, and I didn't "look sick," so they never found any resolution to my problem.

Even while I was thinking such horrid things about food and about my body, I still genuinely thought it was a fault only in myself. I didn't pay attention to others' bodies. I clarify because I understand that it can be frustrating when a thin person complains about body dysmorphia and eating disorders. There is nothing about what I thought or how I behaved that was healthy, and it is something I still struggle with, although my relationship with my body and with food has improved significantly.

I was so eager to get away from my peers and my city. Again, I loved my friends and family: finding yourself and wanting to explore and see different places and experience different things does not mean you do not love and appreciate the people you are moving away from. I always craved adventure and freedom. My city would not satisfy me, so I knew I had to leave, which instilled an early desire of mine to be older. I remember my mom excitedly told our neighbor, on my tenth birthday, that I was "finally in the double digits." I wished I had turned forty; forty was closer to sustainable independence than ten, and I was impatient (I still am impatient, but forty is much closer now). I finished high school in three years and then traveled across the country for college. I was paired with an amazing roommate who remains a very beloved friend of mine. I'm sure I wasn't the easiest to be around, as I was awkward, anxious, and closed. She, unfortunately, had to witness the beginnings of my disastrous melancholy.

My mental anguish was brewed and simmering by January of 2011, and, over the course of that year, it spilled and flooded and stained until, on December 8, 2011, I received my first 5150.

I had anxiety, insomnia, depression, dysphoria, disordered eating, and terrifying bouts of mania. I was delusional. Psychosis left me talking to my hallucinated monsters, which would so eagerly talk back. I named them and laughed with them and would often feel them lift me by my ankles and drop me down onto my bed. My hallucinations encompassed me. I ate only small servings of rice and ground ginger.

My daydreams consumed me. In high school, I trained myself to be a lucid dreamer, which helped me to be better able to stay more coherent when I drifted off within my mind. But there was no longer any significant border between fantasy and reality, and I wasn't able to identify any piece of myself that I didn't want to destroy.

I tried many medications and have been to multiple psychiatrists and therapists. I was hospitalized. I went off meds, went back on meds, changed up meds, went off meds, went back on meds; I stopped self harming and then started self harming and then stopped self harming: a long cycle that started to feel repetitive, tiresome, and, too often, devastatingly fruitless. Healing is not linear, and I am learning to not allow my relapses to devastate me as strongly as they once did.

It is harder than it ever should be to find decent mental health care. You often have to prove you are "sick enough" to get help; you get pushed around by offices and doctors so much until it becomes so much of a struggle that it is difficult to not give up looking for help entirely. It can take years of different doctors and programs to finally find the perfect medicine, and the times before and in between can be insane, furious, and sorrowful. When you look back, it can feel like a memory of someone entirely separate. In the midst of one of my melancholies, during which I became even more dismayed against the mental health care system, I realized that those who can receive decent help in a reasonable time had to have both money and an abundance of free time.

I spent about a decade incorrectly diagnosed with Bipolar 2. I'm quiet and well-mannered; I take things out on myself rather than on others, which goes against common Borderline Personality Disorder stereotypes. It's frustrating. Maddening, really (ha!). There are many ways that disorders manifest, and not all of them are obvious, textbook examples. I learned how difficult it is to get a BPD diagnosis, and that, even if you do manage to get the diagnosis, so many doctors specifically single BPD out as something they will not treat. I know that so many people with BPD had to self-diagnose because, overall, the doubt and stigma that surrounding the illness encouraged it to be swept under the medical rug or misdiagnosed as something else.

Over the next several years, my mental health improved, but I did have minor hiccups and some brief inpatient stays. I'd fluctuate with self harm, and cutting, in particular, became very regular for me again by the end of 2017. I struggled with alcoholism. I continued to fight my body. My most recent melancholy occurred in the summer of 2020. My symptoms were surprisingly unrelated to COVID, although the pandemic did aid in the difficulty of communicating adequately with medical professionals. I took a leave from work to pursue medical treatment. I tried to document my turmoil, but my musings, instead of contenting my mind through attempted reflection, often increased my intoxicating disgust for my situation. I felt resentment, rage, and misery. I set my words aside and tried to find emotional balance. The warmth and support from loved ones helped thin my melancholy; its veil was still heavy, but I saw freckles of light through it, and I could still breathe. I quit Xanax (which I was addicted to for over a decade), stopped regularly self-harming, and am no longer dependent on alcohol. I found a fantastic psychiatrist who helped me figure out my perfect medicinal cocktail.

It took three decades, but I found a balance.

It was always an ambition of mine to share my words with the world– to invite others into both my sorrows and my joys, and so I will begin:

Once Upon a Time, there loomed Emily Carol, 17, and in their Freshman year of college...

Magickal Morose and the Meddlesome Melancholy

1/25/11

I assume that everyone doesn't like me. It's safer that way.

P.S. I really want to die.

1/25/11

Time. Time. Time. Numbers. Prime numbers. People. Faces. Smiles. Smirks. Sneers. Lies. Falsity. Anger. Disappointment.

I just want to sleep. But I can't. There's so much to do. My skin is terrible and I'm becoming quite fat. People dislike me– it's obvious. I feel alone and depressed, and everything is breaking. I just want to sleep. I've disappointed myself and seem to disappoint my teachers/grandparents/bosses/colleagues, etc... I can't stop freaking out about time. TIME. TIME. TIME. I just want to be 37, living on my own, writing, separated from these false, rude people. I want to show people I am someone– I'm not spineless or weak...or am I? I want to die.

1/25/11

Emily, whenever you are, talk to me, please. I am so lonely. I want someone to be close to. I hope you are happy. Please talk to me...you are the only one with whom I can be completely honest with.
Why am I talking to myself?

1/27/11

Emily, I am not feeling much better. But I went to the nurse and will be seeing the counselor in half an hour. I hope he helps. I got sweetarts in the mail, so I'm not feeling as down as I normally am. Keep me posted.

1/31/11

He was nice.
I think I'm going to drop that Chinese class.

2/1/11

I sometimes feel like I'm acting all the time. I'm the comic relief. It can be exhausting. No one wants me to be sad because it's troublesome, yet they can be as emotional as they want. Lucky bastards.

2/4/11

I feel really shitty today. I'm beginning to realize that I'm just a convenience. People only do things with me if it benefits them or if they have nothing else to do. That's all I am: the convenient comic relief. People don't hang out with me just to hang out with me.

I'm failing at everything.

And I'm tired all the time.

And no one really cares.

2/6/11

Last night I dreamt about a magical man who liked to hurt people. But he fell in love with a girl, but she was sucked into a wormhole and sent to the future. She found him (dying without her), and when he saw her, his magic returned and his health and young-ish age were restored. (People kept warning her that he would hurt her, but he never did.)

3/6/11

Nobody genuinely likes me.

I'm just a convenience.

I really want to die.

6/4/11

I want to die.

Right now.

I'm just a convenience; no one really likes me. I'm selfish. I'm gluttonous. I'm stupid. I'm unmotivated. I'm lazy. I don't care about what I should care about. I'm paranoid. I'm fucking ugly. No matter what, nobody notices me. I'm disgusting, and I want to sleep all the time, but can't. I can't connect with people— once I befriend them, I just want to hide, yet I hate it when people ignore me. I'm tired of condescension and fake smiles.

So I should die.

I also hate that I think I'm different from everyone else. I'm not; I'm an ordinary teenager (except I find it is very difficult for me to cry).

So I must turn to the knife.

And I hate how unemotional I am around people, yet I hate giving in to emotions.

STUPID FATASS WITH STUPID HAIR.

7/4/11

     I have a new friend. Her name is Bridget. She is orange and has delightfully sharp fingernails. <3 We will have so much fun together! She makes everything so much less stressful.

7/4/11

     I feel sick whenever I eat anything. I'm beginning to really hate food. It's disgusting.

8/11/2011

     I dreamed that I met Socrates. And then I transferred to a school in Athens to study philosophy.

9/28/11

     I cut a lot today. And I punched and slapped myself in the face. I'm fat. And I'm not in school. I really hate myself. I'm an ugly girl surrounded by beautiful, smart people. It's too warm; they're going to see the scars. My room is the only place where I feel safe.

9/29/11

     I keep having annoying mood swings. I go from feeling ecstatic to feeling like killing myself. And I have difficulty ignoring this urge to cut. Especially when I think about how much I am burdening everyone with my medical "problems." I can't schedule my health around the insurance companies. However, I guess I should be proud of myself: I didn't cut, even though the urge was so strong today. I think the only thing that helps is talking to people on mental health forums. They are similar, and so they understand. And so I will try my best. Right now both my thighs, stomach, and both upper arm areas are covered. Last night the cuts on my stomach bled through my nightgown. Lovely.

9/30/11 1:11 PM

     I just cut myself again. And now I'm going to lie on my bed and try to ignore the fact that I'm sweating and hot when the air is on. I really hate things right now. And I just ate and feel like a fat ass pig. I was planning on just having dinner (a little bit, even though that's the worst time of day to eat), but I'm a fatass with no willpower. Someone should poison my next meal.

9/30/11 2:23 PM

I feel a little better. I have some new ideas for art/stories. I still don't have the motivation to do it, though. How long until this feeling goes away and I feel completely numb again? Hmm...

9/30/11 2:26 PM

Okay. Now I want to fucking dance around the house like a moron. But I wonder, if I do that, how hard the crash will be.

9/30/11 3:08 PM

I think I would be better off being with other people who are like me. Like the people online. I feel like I can be so open with them. They understand and accept, and that is a relief to me.

9/30/11 3:46 PM

I am still feeling okay. My cuts are stinging, and my pelvic area is hurting (still don't know why). I want to create so many things, but I can't get myself to start working on them. And I know I should do a better job looking for jobs, but I am afraid. What if I have a sudden mood swing? What will I say or do? I'm terrified of social interaction. How the hell can I deal with customers?

9/30/11 4:55 PM

Suddenly I feel like crap. Irritated. Angry. I want to cut or die.

9/30/11 5:11 PM

Suddenly fatigued. Depressed. I want to hit myself and die. The thought of dying comforts me. I am going to cut...how long until I run out of space on my skin? I feel fat. And stupid and ugly. And it's too hot in my room.

9/30/11 6:10 PM

Depressed and in pain. It hurts to walk and sit. Hey, at least I'm feeling something.

9/30/11 8:31 PM

Randomly ecstatic (though still in pain). Going to bake cookies.

9/30/11 Sometime after 11 PM

I am okay. I ate a cookie earlier and immediately felt like a fat pig. But, then again, I AM a fat pig. I have grown a habit of taking nightly baths. I feel as if I am washing the horrid day off (for every day is quite horrid) and I give my cuts a thorough cleaning, for my intent is that they heal, not damage, me.

9/30/11

I feel very numb. It's like I'm blank. There is nothing but the desire to cut and die. My pelvic area has been hurting for about a month now, and I hate not knowing why. But I'd feel embarrassed going to the doctor about it. Plus we can't really afford it. I already used all our medical money. I just had another cutting binge. It didn't really help my mood; I still feel numb. And I noticed that the cuts aren't bleeding as much as they usually do. I like to see blood. I wonder if it's because I'm dehydrated...

I'm going to have to pick a designated journal eventually. I've been writing in at least three different ones.

Well. I want to cut.

Tata.

Well. Goodnight. (I will fight this urge to stay awake.)

Oh, however much I wish to lock my door at night (for if someone entered, they would see my cuts), I leave it unlocked in the event that I am overcome with a need to kill myself. That way they can find me without having to break the door down.

It's midnight. I must take my pills and rest.

10/2/2011 (Dreams)

Boyfriend? Leaves. I turn male, hire a prostitute (my ex-bf comes back and hides in the closet with the prostitute).

There is a riot in the streets. Parade of people and giant slugs (the government) and civilians who stand their ground are corralled into a "palace." People who get in the way continually are dissolved by giant slug things. I am lined up with others on the side and then am taken to an observation area (I had my blood drawn and was "interviewed"). I see I'm favored, and this really angers one of the guards. At one point, I run away and go into a closet with a partial ladder to the ceiling that leads to the other prisoners, but I cannot reach it regardless of my climbing up boxes, and I fall, knocking things over. Angry guard hears and opens the closet door, finding me on the floor.

10/2/11 11:57 AM

I forgot to write yesterday. I was in an okay mood. I did cut though (however, I find that I cut regardless of my mood). Today I feel okay, yet feel a wave of depression coming. I think I may go on another cutting binge soon.

10/2/11 6:50 PM

Super. Fucking. Depressed. I didn't eat much, and followed my sister to Walmart. Couldn't make up my mind whether to stop at Michaels to get canvas and small, wooden coffin...knew self was getting hungry, but also knew I HATE going anywhere when my stomach is full. Felt like dying. Kinda planned it out. Then went home and cut and felt a lot better. I am now using razor blades instead of knives– so much better! Am going to the store to get more cutting supplies tonight.

Am excited.

10/2/11 10:05 PM

Walked to Walgreens after dinner (despite my hating going anywhere directly after eating). Bought a ton of bandages and gauze pads, medical tape, and alcohol wipes. Oh, and two mini first-aid kits. Spent nearly $20, but don't feel nearly as guilty as I do when I spend money on other things. Still feeling a little suicidal, but knowing I have a clean, safe, and handy dandy "cutting kit," I'm not as...tempted. My pelvic area still hurts a bit, and I still am not sure why. But I've noticed that whenever I cut, my anxiety and panic (usually felt towards not knowing why I am hurting) is lessened, and I find I am able to (although not much) relax just a bit. And it helps that my clown is always at my side. And venting to people online has helped so much. (I named my razor blade Esther.)

10/3/11 11:14 AM

Kinda regret buying all those bandages. Hopefully, I will return them today...then I'll have more money to buy laughing coffins.

10/3/11 11:31 AM

I feel so fucking gross and ugly right now. I am such a fat, stupid loser. Why am I so afraid to go anywhere?

10/4/11 8:46 PM

I didn't cut yesterday, but I ended up cutting today. One large "patch" and one small "patch." Haven't had severe mood swings today, but did have some moments of panic. I may not be granted a single room for next semester, and that is the only way I will feel able to go back to school.

10/5/11 10:57 AM
Feeling extremely creative today,

10/5/11 7:25 PM
Was feeling okay all day.
Suddenly hit with something, and am now feeling extremely depressed. I was painting, too. Painting usually makes me happy. I need to cut.

Cut a giant patch. I can't tell if the stains on my hands are from blood or from paint. I want to stop, but I love it. It's the only thing keeping me alive.

I really want to die. I'm fat and ugly and my face is crooked. I quit everything, I'm scared of people, I hate everything, I'm jealous, I'm stupid, I'm selfish, and I deserve to bleed to death. I don't even deserve to die in my sleep, though the thought of overdose tempts me.

10/5/11 8:19 PM
The smell of blood was so strong today.

10/5/11 11:19 PM
I hate everything. I want to die. And organize. And clean. And scream. And cut. I'm too pathetic for my own good. People will only realize that I've deactivated my account on Facebook just because my stupid posts and face won't be spamming their newsfeeds. I'm always on the verge of a panic attack. I panic about panicking. I'm scared of people. I'm a germaphobe. I am OBSESSED with time and numbers and counting, and I have to constantly make sure the oven and dryer are off, fridge closed. Things have to FEEL right when I do them, or I have to repeat and repeat and repeat and repeat and repeat and repeat and repeat and repeat.
Repeat as much as the scratches on my body. Line after line after line after line after line of red tears.

10/7/11 11:05 PM
Didn't cut today.

10/8/11 12 AM

What I Need To Work On:

Self Mutilation: Cutting; hitting; scratching. I don't have much annoyance towards this besides how difficult it is to dress "appropriately." My cuts keep me from death, so I do view them as my friends, but the rest of society cannot understand this. Yes, I am suicidal, and whenever that urge is super strong, all I can do is lie in bed and wish for death and imagine how to do it and plan when and where. Then I can turn to the cuts. They save me more than they harm me. And on that note: I do feel suicidal. I am not sure why. I feel like there is a voice inside me coaxing me. Yet I have learned that much of this is caused by chemical imbalances in the brain. What can I do to even things out? Cutting works, but the voices come back in waves. Voices, cut, fine, voices, cut, voices, cut, cut, fine, fine, cut, cut (addicted, you see), voices, cut, etc... And of course, suicide is also viewed negatively by society. Personally, I think people should have control over their own lives. Why make me suffer just so you can be at ease? Let me go.

Anxiety/Fear/Panic: I often can't explain why I am so scared. I don't want to leave the house, go to the store, to the gym, anywhere, not even to be with "friends" (I view many as "acquaintances" because I'm too socially awkward and inept to make friends). I hate physical contact and opening up emotionally. I'm usually just the comic relief, the amusing one. I get panic attacks thinking about panic attacks, and every possible health risk frightens me (and yet I am still suicidal). This makes no sense.

Depression: I can't describe how I feel at my lowest. I'm numb. I can't do anything. It's not even a matter of "won't" or "don't want to." I physically and mentally can't. And it comes in cycles, like (and I know this isn't an original description) a rollercoaster. It hits and I am incapable of doing anything to stop it. Sure, cutting often makes me feel better, and keeps me from death, but sometimes I can't even cut because I'm not motivated enough to move. The most I want to do is reach, pick up my pills, and swallow all of them. And that's when I begin to bargain again. "Oh, well, let's give it a week. If things don't get better in a week, you can just kill yourself. Yes." Or, "well, if things don't go well this year, I can just kill myself." Where do these thoughts come from? Don't know. But they're loud.

Back to panic: at one moment, after my second ER trip (all panic related), this Summer, I hadn't slept in a while (this reminds me: I must talk about insomnia later), I felt I was in a constant state of panic, and I was ...hallucinating? I'll admit to seeing things occasionally. Who doesn't? Who doesn't also hear their name called? Or hear music loud and clear although there is nowhere for it to be coming from? Well, as I lay on my bed, freaking out, I eventually felt relief as I decided (and it made perfect sense) that I was simply being visited by monsters (they told me their names were Spencer and Chelsea). I had a conversation with them. I thought to them, and they thought back, although I heard their voices out loud in my head. Then they lifted me by my ankles from the bed until I was perpendicular to the mattress. Then they dropped me. When I landed, my body flushed with heat; I became chilly (despite my sweating) and I smiled and laughed and floated and giggled and conversed. And out loud told myself, "Monsters! That's it!" Then, finally, I slept for a couple of hours. When I woke up, I was confused, amused, and, since I was still not recovered from my seemingly permanent state of panic, very, very afraid.

     I mentioned earlier about insomnia. I have had many nights where I couldn't sleep at all and many more where, if I do sleep, I always wake up between 1 AM and 4 AM on the hour. My days felt so long. When I woke up, my mind would be racing and I'd have to get up, shower, get coffee, and work on something or listen to music and pace. Maybe it's this obsession with time that I have always had. I'm obsessed with numbers (my favorite being odd primes), and I count and have to be early for everything. And I get so anxious before going anywhere that I must prepare hours early and sit and wait, even if it means waiting all day. Whenever I am dealing with time, I panic. And I must always get sleep. I am obsessed with sleep because it is difficult to achieve. I plan for nine hours, and get super anxious as my bedtime approaches (I gave it to myself). I honestly begin counting down the hours until I can sleep when I wake up (maybe I look forward to my vivid and often lucid dreams?). Either way, my time/sleep anxiety drives me crazy.

10/9/11 12:01 AM

     I did not cut today/yesterday! Although I still feel the urge and do (still) not view it as "evil", I am proud, as the cuts get very, very itchy when they begin to heal. I have two social outings tomorrow (today, I guess). I will be facing acquaintances for the first time in weeks. I hope I don't panic or fall into one of my random moods. This should be interesting.

10/9/11 12:04 AM

     With wings too small to fly, why bother to survive?

10/9/11 12:12 AM

     I am scared of ending up all alone, yet I fear socializing, physical contact, and bonding (even with people who consider me their good friend). Once I get to a certain point in a friendship, I get scared and no longer wish to see them...but yet I miss them, but do not want to visit them or for them to visit me.

10/10/11 2:51 PM

Was feeling okay for the past couple days, then today I fell back into my "dark mood." I hate this. And what makes it worse is that I felt it coming. And I couldn't do anything about it. I took a shower and cut, but not as much as I wanted to, however; I am running out of healed, easily hidden skin. And to cut where people can see will end with my receiving rude, ignorant, and hateful comments.

10/10/11 4:01 PM

So full of rage. I want to cut it out of me.

10/10/11 4:45 PM

I am having one of those moments (should it really be called a "moment?" It lasts a lot longer) where I HATE everything. Watching a child play outside from my window makes me want to fucking murder something, or cut myself, or scream. Watching a man go to his car and drink his stupid soda disgusts me. It's like there is something inside me that is flowing throughout my body and making me sick with hatred and disgust and anger. I need to cut it out of me. How will I survive college like this. The constant ups and downs will surely lead me to kill myself, for when I would go for my walks, that was all I thought about: jumping off of that beautiful, rocky cliff.

10/10/11 8:33 PM

Was feeling absolutely miserable earlier, and cut my thighs a good bit. Felt a little better, though still "numb." But suddenly, several moments later, I felt okay. Although my annoyance meter is still pretty high (I feel as if anyone or anything who/that does one thing that annoys me will reactivate this rage that seems to be living inside of me. Occasionally bled out with my red tears). I feel as though another bout of "darkness" is coming, and am not looking forward to it. I foresee my body covered in scars, and always having at least one patch of fresh cuts. I worry (is it really worrying though? Because it feels more like longing, like I will finally be able to scratch an eighteen year old itch) that I may one day be unable to control my blade and will cut too deep. Oh, what a mess there shall be!

Oh! And although I have never considered myself a night person, I find that I am most productive late at night/early in the morning. When I was in school, I would wake up between the hours of one and four in the morning, and would feel a need to get up and pace, work, listen to music, shower, drink tea...basically start my day. And yet I am a morning person. An *early* morning person. That would make sense, seeing as those hours are technically early morning...

~And the thoughts, they never stop~

10/11/11 4:24 PM

I was feeling remarkably okay today; I had a random hour of pure, ecstatic dancing in the family room, much to the amusement of my cats and dog. I thought I would cut (for even when I am feeling my best, I have the urge to cut. Addiction. Lovely, lovely addiction), but, to my surprise, I didn't. Even after I had taken my ritualistic shower during which I cleaned my already existing cuts, I decided against cutting. Perhaps I am that desperate to preserve my skin. How long until I completely stop caring whether or not people can see my scars and cuts? Many people flaunt (or at least, poorly hide) their addictions, so why should I hide? Yes, I guess to some it can be deemed "unsightly." But I believe that scars are better than polluted lungs or damaged livers, and my recreational activity does not physically affect others (as does secondhand smoke).

Moving on from that subject: today is my first visit with a counselor. I am currently waiting (for I have arrived an hour early. Damn this obsession and anxiety with time!) and already think that this therapy will prove useful to me. I also observed a girl, perhaps twelve or thirteen, waiting as well. She was reading and making notes in the margins, and was wearing a delightful pink and green tutu. I felt so comfortable waiting here with her, which is a rare thing. But I wonder: why is it that so many people who are mentally unstable appear intelligent and creative? Is it at all possible that our illnesses are not deficiencies; maybe we have received, somehow (for I believe in no God) a higher capacity for both artistic clarity and artistic reason (what does that even mean?). Anyway, the girl went into the office with her mother, and I now sit alone, ocean sounds emitting from what appears to be an alarm clock. I'm wondering if I will finally get more than a "you need to work on anxiety," for I believe there is more going on inside this head of mine. I'm just never given enough time to describe things. Also, I tend to forget what it is I plan to bring up in my brief visits with my psychiatrist/doctor, and only have time for them to prescribe me some new medication sure to screw up my system and nauseate me (although, I must admit that I am tolerant of Xanax). Will someone actually work with me to fix these problems, or will they do the usual shaking of the head, in their obvious disapproval of me, and announce that I should magically just stop my habits altogether?

As if I can pour all my worries and thoughts and habits into a bottle whenever they probe too stressful or "dangerous." HA!

Imma draw now:

ONWARDS from my doodling. I'd rather be depressed by the truth than enlightened by a lie. And who is to say that depression itself cannot be enlightening? People who never go through certain experiences do not understand. So why are we always viewed negatively? Why must we be judged by society, while the ignorant are (seemingly) encouraged to remain ignorant? It's frustrating. Which is why I will never view suicide as a negative thing, for I understand the desire to leave this polluted planet and the many people who infest it. No, I don't believe in heaven (however, the fact that energy cannot be created or destroyed leaves me with the thought that I could possibly be transported, my mind at least, to another dimension. But since I have no way of testing that theory ((unless I were to die)), I can only leave it as a simple meandering thought), and so when I think of death, I imagine the most amazing sleep ever. The longing for it is so strong: I can imagine the feeling of the blade cutting my wrist. I will bleed to death, and, as I become weaker, will become sleepier and sleepier, and, knowing this time that I can sleep (without my drugs even!), I will be so happy, so satisfied, so content. I will slip away, smile on my face, relieved to finally be free. Oh, writing about it makes me crave it so much. Yet I know I will mask this craving by cutting once I get home. Maybe the skin on my upper thigh is healed just enough to bleed again. Oh, how does my mind always wander back to killing myself and cutting? It must mean I'm committed.

10/11/11 10:49 PM

I really like my new therapist. She is nice, and enjoys art and writing. I found that I was in a much more pleasant mood after the session, although I still have a strong urge to cut. But I noticed that I was more positive on Facebook and have been "counseling" some fellow mentally ill friends online. It actually makes me feel good to help people who are dealing with similar (not the same, however, for no situations are the same) issues that I went/am going through.

10/12/11 2:26 PM
    Feel better than usual, yet ended up cutting a lot. I am still having trouble deciding which college I should attend; half of me is lured by the artsy and super relaxed open-mindedness of Warren Wilson, and the other half of me is yearning for something super prestigious and structured. I don't know what I should do! I love writing. I have always known that that's what I want to spend the rest of my life doing. But which school would better serve me? SCAD or WWC? Or should I apply to Emory or Yale (they have been haunting me for some time). I don't want to use up all my college money. I have already used a fourth of it, so it would make sense to return to WWC, right? Then I can continue on track as if I never took time off. Maybe I can even finish in Spring 2013. That would be so lovely. I've made some pro/con lists and they don't seem to be helping. And I have no idea if I'll get put on a good crew or get my single room in a nice dorm. Ah! I wish it weren't so difficult for me to make important decisions that will influence the rest of my life. Of course, WWC does have the circus, which was the only thing that kept me from jumping off a cliff or dropping out of school last Spring.

    I wish I knew what to do.

    I also really want to go to that clown camp! But I can't see how it would be possible. I'd need nearly $1,400. Hmm...

10/12/11 3:09 PM
    Looks like I'm leaning towards Warren Wilson.

10/12/11 5:21 PM
    I've noticed that I've felt more positive today than I have in a long time. Maybe it's because I have a therapist who I know is going to help me (free me). I'm actually looking forward to the day ahead which is something I haven't felt in a long time. Most nights I go to sleep hoping I won't wake up in the morning. While I'll admit that I enjoy being thought of in a positive way, I still fear getting close to people. I don't trust them. I don't want people to know about what I like and what I do; it's personal to me. The more they know about me, the easier it is for them to hurt me. I wish I could get over this fear of friendship and human contact. Maybe then I would be able to better present myself and not appear only as an awkward geek with bad acne and bushy eyebrows. I'm so confused. Ha! What a generic thing to write in a diary! Oh, how I long to cut right now.

10/12/11 6:56 PM

Not quite depressed, but not happy, yet not numb. Hmm. I want to bleach the hell out of my hair and dye it purple, and I want to hula hoop and make fun outfits and write a play and perform it. All tonight. Maybe I should look into those things. Or devote my entire day to working on a story. Which story, though? There are so many characters and plots trying to get out of my head. Maybe that's why I cut. I must bleed out in order to make room inside my body for new ideas.

I really wish I could just be a clown.

10/12/11 7:40 PM

I think I have finally thought of a way to describe this pain I've been feeling over the past couple of months: it feels like there are a bunch of unsurfaced boils all over my pelvic area/upper thighs. It hurts to sit, walk, and stand. But I'm too embarrassed to bring it up to anyone. Ouch.

Oh geez; this is the worst feeling ever. Maybe I'll mention it to the G.I., although it really has nothing to do with him, and I don't like him very much.

I want to hula hoop.

10/12/11 7:45 PM

Oh! I've thought of a good solution to my cutting dilemma (running out of hidden space)! If I just start wearing my stockings more often, I won't have to worry about them being seen. I'm surprised I haven't thought of this before. It's quite the obvious solution. This is something to keep in mind should I ever return to school, which I suspect I will be doing in January. Haha!

A solution.

Ahahaha.

And, lucky me, I have so many socks to choose from!

Time to cut.

10/12/11 9:14 PM

I managed not to cut after my shower, which was what I was planning to do and why I took my shower in the first place. I guess that it's good; although the desire is still strong.

10/12/11 9:23 PM

I've been thinking about what I want for my first tattoo to be. I think a pin-up clown would be cool, with a futuristic look. And maybe a tabby cat with wings, resembling freedom and independence. I've thought about the sphinx cat (from *Mirrormask*). Or one of my mushroom people, or even Sunkist. Ha! Or that awesome Sylvia Plath quote that I love so much.

10/13/11 11:41 AM

So...I'm on the waitlist for a single room. I can (possibly, maybe, most likely not) get a single in The Village (of course they'd stick me with three random people who are sure to dislike me...). Or I can have a roommate in Wellness. I guess if I weren't a recluse, I wouldn't have such a problem with having a roommate, but it just causes so much anxiety for me~ The anticipation that someone will come in at any moment keeps me from doing anything productive, letting my guard down, sleeping, eating, doing anything. I understand that my requests are very far fetched to many, but to me they are needed, not wanted. I will go crazy. I will fling myself off of that beautiful, rocky ledge, certainly. I need solitude, for it helps me muster up enough courage to socialize (which sounds strange, but nevertheless it is true). Oh please! Please, housing people who hold my future in your hands. Please give me a single room! I promise you will never see or hear from me again, for I will spend all my time in my room. Ha! Well, at least now I have another thing to worry about.

I want to cut and scream and fucking destroy something.

10/13/11 12:32 PM

I wish that not everyone would hate me. I know I'm not nice, pretty, or cool...

10/13/11 12:48 PM

Maybe if I organize my "arguments" well, I will be granted a single room. Hmm... (I use "hmm.." a lot). Let's see...well:

- I have terrible anxiety and panic problems.
- I self mutilate (especially when under stress, and living with people causes great stress).
- I am depressed.
- I am shy.
- I am introverted.
- I manage my emotions much better when given a place where I am guaranteed solitude.
- I can't sleep around people, even when on medication...it makes me panic.
- I have time/sleep anxiety (I guess the same as above).

- I can be sure to be composed around other people because I have time to "prepare" for social interactions.
- I need a safety zone.

I will continue the list later. Thinking about this is making me panic. Must take more Xanax.

10/13/11 1:08 PM

It's pathetic how I panic just at the thought of not having a single room. Had to take a Xanax and I'll be fixing a cup of earl grey in a moment. I really want to cut, but am becoming a bit weirded out by the smell that accompanies it: smells like blood and flesh, obviously, but it is so strong and it lingers on my clothes and in my bed... must transform cutting urge into tea urge. Ugh.

I hate you, Jeffrey Panic!

10/13/11 2:16 PM

I want to be a writer, an artist, an actress, a singer, a performer, a circus clown, and a traveler.

10/13/11 3:32 PM

I am getting my bout of nausea that usually hits me three or four times a day. Although I am not sure what causes it. And my wisdom teeth/TMJ pain does not help. It feels like someone is pressing a hammer on my jaw and the back of my eyes. And the pain radiates. I went to cut and get myself to focus on something else, but I really, really want to fight the urge, which is hard to do since I don't view cutting as a negative thing.

10/13/11 5:21 PM

Oh, I am such a disgusting loser. I'm going nowhere in life. Disappointment. So much disappointment.

10/13/11 8:11 PM

Thinking about rooms again and panicking. I can't have a roommate. I can't. It isn't a matter of want. I can't. And I really need to get a job, but my anxiety holds me back, and I'm too stubborn to remove my piercings because I'm a loser that way, but I really want to attend the clowning arts camp; I feel it would really help me come out of my shell. And I hope to one day be in charge of writing the WWC circus, and having that clowning background would be so lovely! Oh, how I love clowns.

Clowning is the only thing that kept me from dropping out of college and jumping off that beautiful, rocky ledge.

10/13/11 8: 29 PM

I want to run away and join the circus.

10/13/11 10:04 PM

I WILL get a job. Why? So that I can go to the awesome clowning arts camp.

10/13/11 11:33 PM

I attempted to make gluten free cupcakes. Made icing, which I ate a lot of. I feel so nauseous. Ahhh. I need salt. And I need to lose tons of weight. Blegh.

10/14/11 1:06 PM

I just thought I'd write just for the sake of writing. I'm really wanting to pursue the clowning arts camp, but I'm also hoping to pull together a short play (or at least finish writing my Artificial Intelligence story) before going back to WWC.

10/15/11 1:59 PM

Just cut. I hate being left out of things and I hate that I am not flexible and I hate that I always QUIT everything, and so I'm mediocre at everything I do. I want to cut more, but it will take longer to clean up. MUST AVOID WRISTS. Although death doesn't sound bad at all. I won't feel my weight when I'm dead. I want to vomit and bleed out all of the stupidity and anger and jealousy that poisons me. Maybe then I would have some fucking self confidence.

CUT CUT SLICE SLICE OOOH THAT FEELS SO NICE CUT SLICE BLEED BLEED BLEED OUT ALL THAT POISONS ME

"Smile Like You Mean It" —Ironic that I'm listening to that right now.

10/15/11 2:13 PM

I had been having a good couple of days, but suddenly fell back into this... "darkness" (only stereotypical description I could think of). And why the hell do they make bandages so sticky that they rip the skin when pulled away? Kinda defeats the purpose of the band-aid. I want to be happy and confident and productive but I can't because I feel crappy and sick and stupid and fat and jealous. My hair is greasy and my acne is horrid. And I constantly smell of blood and cut skin, and the stench takes over everything that I touch. And I am dreading returning to school because I know people there don't like me. Why the hell should they? I am not a nice person: I'm reclusive and anxious and prone to panic for the silliest of reasons. I'm judgmental and awkward and ugly and cold and distant and snobby. I complain too much, like weird things, and am too obsessed with how fucked up the government (and humans in general) are. I need money, yet am too scared to get a job. And I will spend my money, not on education, but on clowning, because all I do is drop everything and join the fucking circus because that's the only thing that would make a foolish child like me happy. And to think I've wanted to be forty years old since I was ten, yet I can't even handle everyday stresses that everyone else just deals with and I can't sleep because I'm paranoid and I turn to blades instead of tears. And I just want to die, yet I don't want to go before my stories are heard because I'm full of myself and want everyone to see that I am fucking capable of some things. But I'm too lazy to finish anything. And so I sit and cut and eat and not eat and wish I were what I'm too scared to become and complain to everyone about every little thing because I am a loser. I should just die! I have Esther. One slice, and I'm gone. I'm so reclusive, no one will think to check on me, which gives me perfect time to bleed out. But then there will be stains to clean, and my family is already in debt, although a funeral is far cheaper than a fucking college education and clown camp and gluten free, dairy free food, and pomegranate juice.

I really hate myself.

10/15/11 4:53 PM

I just feel so numb today. Was dropped off early because I no longer felt like grocery shopping. Cut a large patch in my thighs. Debating whether or not to go see *The Illusionist*, a play. The thought of being in public and around people makes me want to sleep. My cuts keep bleeding.

10/16/11 12:05 PM

Oh silly me. A hooligan I must be. Thinking, researching, questioning. Clearly I am confused. I've stumbled from the trail, set out for me by others. If I said I'd do anything for you, anything for you, anything for you. Know that I'll be there, that I do care, that I will always love. I'd do anything for you.

10/16/11 4:31 PM

I dropped off my Aaron Brothers app (looking like crap, I might add). I will call the manager tomorrow to maybe set up an interview. Then

I borrowed $20 (in debt, again) to buy a long, straight, burgundy wig. I'm pleased, although not very used to having long hair. And I hope it's not easily tangled.

10/16/11 5:06 PM
Why do I want a job? I want to go to clown camp, get a tattoo, and see live shows. I need money.

And have I mentioned how much I love clowns.

10/16/11 9:38 PM
Managed not to cut today. Felt like it, though (when do I not feel like cutting?). Am beginning to panic because it sounds like this guy wants to hang out with me. I'm definitely not cool enough for him. I don't drive, I don't smoke, I can't drink, I'm vegetarian, and I'm allergic to everything. I'm a pro-gay feminist anime geek, and I have no conversation skills. I don't like staying out late and I have no money. I've never dated, never kissed, and never had sex. I'm just not cut out for this whole "socializing" thing, let alone dating thing. I won't know how to react to him. Or his friends. Goodness, why can't people leave me alone? Oh, wait, I feel excluded when they do. Yet I don't like feeling obligated to hang out with or entertain them. I really am just a bad person. No fun. Not cool. Just an awkward nerd. Who buys wigs with money she doesn't have. I just want to run away, abandon all my connections (not forever, but for a while), join the circus, write, and create. Let me slip into my dreams and be free. Please, just please, don't force me to live this reality.

10/16/11 10:28 PM
I. Am. A. Fat. Ass.

10/17/11 1:26 PM
Not depressed. Was terribly estatic a moment ago, and have tons of creative ideas running through my head. I want to write and draw and film so many things; I have so many stories to share and bring to life.

10/17/11 2:56 PM
I found my mandala that I made during the first week of CART. On it, I illustrated five goals which I want to meet sometime (hopefully soon, because I don't expect to live very long):
1.   Publish books

2.   Be put in a medically induced coma and have my dreams monitored
3.   Spend a few nights in a haunted location, record, and observe
4.   Stay in a mental ward and observe
5.   Go hang gliding in Austria
        Hmm...I still really want to accomplish these things, yet seeing as I am very lazy and stupid at the moment, I don't feel like I will ever accomplish anything. I just want to run away and do something just BECAUSE. I don't want to plan because planning and knowing something is going to happen makes me exceedingly anxious. Of course, knowing anything can happen at any moment also makes me exceedingly anxious. So, no matter what I do, I will always feel exceedingly anxious. I should just do everything on impulse. Of course, then I'd do what I feel like doing and get in trouble, because my thoughts and wants are not very nice things at all. It's kinda hilarious. I just want a fucking hysterectomy (so I can stop these disgusting periods), and then to run off somewhere, going where I wish and doing as I wish.

10/17/11 3:49 PM
        I feel like I am always acting.
        I don't even know myself.
        And it's hot in here and I'm greasy, fat, and stupid.

10/17/11 3:49 PM
        I am feeling extremely depressed. I just want to cut and sleep. Everything is pointless (cliche, I know, so shut the fuck up about it). I fail at everything. I freak out over things that normally shouldn't bother people. I'm fat. I'm ugly. I'm awkward. I can never finish anything. I have no talents; I am mediocre at everything I do. I lie my way into people's minds. I'm a fake. I don't even know who the real me is. Emily? Carol? Emily Carol? Ambassador Bennet? I play dress up as these characters, yet I don't yet know which ones are real, just as I have trouble figuring out what memories of mine are the truth or the lies I've created within my own mind, with such fluidity, not even I can pick them apart out of my brain. I watch people die in movies and become jealous. I watched a girl almost get hit by a car today and felt angry that she didn't let it hit her— why give up the perfect and rare chance to die without people viewing it, after the fact, as a selfish act? (Hence my always "joking" about being hit by a delivery truck.) And despite this feeling, I still panic about possibly having terminal illnesses, or being around anything that could possibly danger me. Is this just me fearing myself? I don't know. I'll admit, I do fear what will happen

when I no longer am able to control the depth of the cuts or where they happen to go. My wrists, perhaps. That is a fantasy of mine, and I dream of it often. And in dreams, reactions in the brain occur as if the events are actually happening. So is it so impossible that after killing myself over and over and over in my dreams, my brain will view it as a normal habit, and I will do it without thinking? This is one possibility. Oooh, writing this makes me want to cut. I want the blade. Slicey dicey oh so nicely. Ha!

10/17/11 6:59 PM

Basically, I don't think I can trust ANYONE, including myself.
Which of my memories are fake?
Of course, if the stimulation is the same, and they're real to my brain, are they really fake? They didn't happen, but are they fake?
Are they?

10/17/11 8:03 PM

Just cut a good section of my right thigh and the upper part of my left arm. Having a hard time not cutting my left thigh and fat, squishy stomach.
Watching *Hard Candy*. Violent and psychological movies excite and calm me. Thank goodness for them.

10/17/11 9:28 PM

I always feel so much better after watching, reading, and thinking about violent, psychological things. Honestly, I am very excited by things such as this. I have always been. As long as I can remember (yet another cliche) I have been drawn to violence and abuse. Maybe that's why I loved to rent horror films when I was young. Or would feel happy at the thought of punishment. Is this normal? Should I be ashamed? A part of me is, but another part of me thinks, "why the fuck should I care about what others think?!" From what I observe, many, many people have the same fascinations. Why else would there be BDSM? I guess my problem is that I can't be open about it. One reason being that I'm not open with anyone, and another reason being that I don't know of anyone who would understand and accept this– and if I do, they also do a great job at hiding it. Hmm...I guess this explains why I have always drawn extremely violent things and written extremely violent stories. Ha! I'm going to watch more horror/psychological thrillers to cheer myself up. After, of course, I shower and wash these blood stains from my skin.

10/18/11 12:07 PM
    Woke up close to 11am. I hate sleeping in. But my medicine drugs me to sleep, and I am at its mercy until it wears off. But I absolutely hate the feeling of being drugged, and the feeling that I don't have much control while the drugs are in my system. Ugh. And I was frustrated because I couldn't see my therapist at 5:30pm (but we arranged a new time and that's good). It's sad that I look forward to my therapy sessions; they're the only things I look forward to. I had a moment of panic when I saw an acquaintance's post requesting that we should hang out this weekend. I don't want to. I couldn't get myself to respond.
    I have concluded that today is going to suck. It's hot and I'm sweaty and sticky. My skin is gross. Nothing looks right on me. And my closet doors are broken, so I have to battle with them just to find one lousy shirt that won't even cover my cuts properly. And my left headphone doesn't fit properly in my ear, and so it is constantly falling out and feels weird. And I hate today.

10/18/11 3:57 PM
    So. I am feeling a little better– talking with my therapist really does help, and I am eager to actually begin therapy, although I must wait over a week for my next appointment. We finished our "consultation" and she confirmed my anxiety and panic disorder, my depression, my OCD, and (something I had only briefly considered) my bipolar disorder. She called it "Bipolar 2": not as extreme as Bipolar 1, but still extreme. Hmm... I will research this when I get home. She encouraged me to not stop my nightly "serotonin" medicine and also suggested I go on an antidepressant as well as my Xanax. She described it to me very well, from a neuroscience perspective, and I realized that I should at least give it a try. I just hope this doesn't fuck me up as much as the Remeron did. Even my doctor said Remeron "would just fuck you up." I am going to soon be given help to stop overanalyzing everything...that will be nice. And she confirmed: I do need a single room. Ha! WWC better listen, or they may have to deal with a student suicide. Ha! Well, I have many things that I must deal with and learn to work around, but at least I know what they are. I must work on my OCD, anxiety, panic, depression, and bipolar (but how do you fix these things?). Well then. I hope I will have enough time before the beginning of next semester. I don't know how I will fare without therapy if I am not yet "balanced." Perhaps I can see a therapist in NC, but I highly doubt they would take our insurance. And the school's psychologist doesn't really "work with" patients; he just listens and guides (he is nice, but I think I really need more than just guidance). I am tired of my disorders being in

control of me. I want to train them. I want control (this must be a very typical entry for someone dealing with any disorder, compulsion, or addiction. However, it is how I feel).

10/18/11 4:23 PM
Things I want to relearn/learn:
- Cello
- Piano
- Accordion
- Programming
- Flying a plane (or spaceship. Ha!)

10/18/11 8:12 PM
Feel an odd mixture of anger and depression. Why can't people fucking believe me? Just because I don't appear to be bipolar doesn't mean I'm not. I was diagnosed. She said I described it exactly. And besides, I am fake in public; you couldn't know the real me unless you implanted a mind-reading microchip into my brain. It makes sense to me, and I know I shouldn't be bothered by what others think. But really, it is so fucking annoying. They think I'm lying. Lying? Disorders are some of the only things I could never lie about. I do have a habit of faking and putting on a little show for people, though. Why the hell would I ever let anyone know the real me? How fucking dangerous would that be?

I really need to cut. Go to the bathroom, because I am blessed with digestive problems caused from stress (or am I lying about that?) and then cut cut cut cut cut cut. I don't think I deserve to get better, anyways. NC wouldn't be a bad place in which to die.

10/18/11 10:14 PM
Feeling nauseous and have a terrible headache (behind eyes and around ears). I hate this. It comes and goes, but I don't know what it's from. I'm hungry, but I'm too scared to eat because it may make me feel even worse. And I still can't get over how people don't believe that I am bipolar. I guess it shouldn't bother me though. I am who I am, and it shouldn't matter if they can see that. I think I will shower, cut, watch some horror films, and sleep (drugged sleep, of course).

10/19/11 11:50 AM
I'm not really sure how I feel. I am watching a cosmology/physics video, which excites me. If only more people would listen to them. Ah! I can never spell when that stupid serotonin nighty night drug is still in my system. Oh, and I've done more research on bipolar 2 and am happy to

have finally found my disorder (I know that sounds weird). Anyways... I am happy to finally have been given a proper diagnosis.

10/19/11 12:20 PM

I wish I were rich enough to get a degree in Creative Writing, Mathematics, Physics, Philosophy, Psychology, Neuroscience, Music, Computer Science, and Theater. (I'm sure there's more.)

10/19/11 4:07 PM

I'm still feeling neutral right now. I made gluten and dairy free muffins, ate one, and promptly felt disgusting (seriously, I need to lose ten pounds at least). I will do my best not to cut, although my desire to do so is very strong. I'm getting horrendous acne, and am very annoyed. I hope this doesn't become a seasonal thing (last fall, my acne was gross and terrible. The worst it's been). I really need to get going on my clown costume, but have no clue where I should start (and I, unfortunately, don't have the motivation to pursue figuring out a way to start). My head hurts. My ass hurts. My skin is greasy, and I didn't call to refill my propranolol (I only have three pills left...well, four, but I dropped them today and can't find the fourth one). Today sucks. I think I will cut. Or I could just kill myself and it will be quiet.

10/19/11 8:21 PM

I am fucking tired of people assuming that I fake things just because they are "obscure" or "different." I like what I like. I view such things as normal, regardless of whether they're "mainstream" or "underground." If it is interesting to me, I will like it. So these stupid, judgmental assholes should shut the fuck up!

I need to cut now.

10/19/11 8:43 PM

Just cut about half of my upper thigh. It's sad: Sunkist (best cat ever) noticed my cutting and came over and meowed at and sat next to me. I know she does not really understand what I am doing to myself, or how upset I am (or does she?), but it really means a lot. I am only okay with being myself around my cats, and, even then, am I really myself? Half of my memories may be imagined. Do I leave out details from my entries to trick my future mind into forgetting what really has happened? I can't trust myself. I deserve this wonderful, terrible, stinging pain I get when I clean these fresh cuts. I deserve the panic I feel whenever I notice random patches or zits on my skin (ones that are not inflicted by myself), or when I feel this pain on my butt or pelvic area, or the terrible migraines/headaches/whatever the hell this is that hits me, or the nausea that comes all the time, or my insecurities, or my suicidal thoughts. I'm pathetic; I know that. Maybe I can cut the anger and stupidity and fattiness and selfishness out of me. Slice until I die.

10/19/11 10:57 PM

Super depressed. I think tomorrow it's going to hit "full blast." I'm gross, yet I can't stop eating. And at night, too. It's so disgusting to eat before I sleep. And my acne is flaring up. I can see bumps where the acne was this time last year. Oh, I really hope it is not as bad. It's so disgusting. I really do hate myself. I want to die, yet am paranoid of becoming ill. And I'm so itchy. And paranoid. And scared. And gross. And fat. And I want to slice this fat off, or bleed it away. And bleed away this fear and danger and pain. And I want to die, but I want to be in control of my death, which may be why that, while I am suicidal, I always panic about staying healthy and getting every possible threat checked out. Perhaps it is my way of defending myself against my own thoughts and desires. I wish I were happy and beautiful and motivated and confident and loving and social. [But then I don't want to lose my creativity, which I feel is fueled by my "problems." I don't know what to do. If I let myself be treated, I'm afraid a part of myself (a significant part) will be gone. And then I will be bland. But that seems to be what the world wants, and I like the image, but I want to keep my mind, but my mind is what makes me this way. And so I am confused.]

I guess I should call it a night and drug myself to sleep. I feel nauseous.

10/20/11 11:14 AM

Still am not sure how I feel, although I am feeling a bit creative– but that's just because I'm the only one home, and so I can sing and play my keyboard without being heard. It's Anti-Bullying Day. I want to write something for it, but don't know where to start...

To my bullies: Thank you. For pointing out what I need to fix. I'll fix this hair, change my shirt the first moment I get. A chance to revise what has already been made. It's so nice of you to tell me how I must change. Also, thank you for asking if I wanted to die just because of the striped leggings I wore. Your concern was so nice.

I appreciate your putting wet clay on my chair. It's too bad I noticed before I sat, and before you put it in my hair.

I love you for telling me what make-up to wear, regardless of the fact that, then, I really had no care to paint on my face. But I never shared my thoughts. I was too scared of rejection. I knew no one would appreciate my thoughts. Thanks again for laughing at the clothes that I'd wear. Jumping corners, yelling, "freak!" to give me a scare. Mocking my scars and claiming I was insane. Oh! My appreciation for you is so hard to contain.

Seeking me out just to tell me to be someone who you thought people would rather see.

I'm glad you shared your tips, glad I missed school because of it. To go over your words and criticisms. But don't worry. I loved every bit of the delightful teasing, the laughter, the whispers, the lies, which created an experience so strong. A feeling that I needed to come in disguise because of the reception I received from you. When being me made me want to die.

10/20/11 2:53 PM

Why do I feel like I am about to have a panic attack? Why? I took my Xanax like a good girl. So why? My throat feels clogged like I can't breathe. And my teeth hurt. And my skin is still dry. And I think I'm panicking. I hate this.

10/20/11 4:44 PM

Ate and feel crappy. Am finally watching *Saw* 7 in the hopes that it will make me feel better.

10/20/11 7:25 PM

Ate dinner and now feel disgusting (I guess the logical conclusion would be not to eat). I am going to cut (my stomach, since all previous cuts are healed and it is always covered). Feeling incredibly thirsty, but want something fizzy. Anyway. Feeling irritated, fat, and ugly.

10/20/11 7:50 PM

FAT FAT FAT FAT FAT FAT FAT FAT FAT FAT FAT FAT FAT FAT FAT FAT FAT FAT FAT FAT FAT FAT! I am an ugly fatass.

10/20/11 10:16 PM

I just ate again and am such a disgusting fat ass. I am a fat pig who just eats and eats and sits and eats and sits around and does nothing. This is so fucking disgusting. Oh, kill me now, as I am fat and bloated. Give me a fucking grenade and let my fat erupt.

10/21/11 10:42 AM

Feeling okay.

Am worried about going back next semester (all I do is worry, so it's not that unusual, I guess). January, February, and March are what I call "danger" months. I get absolutely depressed during that time. Oh well.

10/21/11 10:54 AM

Feeling super energetic. Want to steal moments.

10/21/11 11:58 AM

Pissed off. Let me cut. I want to see something happen. Ha!

10/21/11 1:11 PM

I should do myself a favor and stop eating.

10/21/11 4:27 PM

Feeling better. Ha. Want to do so many things. So many wonderful, wonderful things. And then I can get hit by a nice truck! Lovely, lovely, lovely! Ha!

10/21/11 7:10 PM

Been in a wonderful mood for the past couple of hours. Baked gluten free, dairy free cupcakes, sang and danced, and even felt motivated to leave the house to take Georgia for a walk. Feel wonderful, violent, sarcastic, although I have a headache (the same kind I've had on and off for a while) and my left eye keeps twitching. Makes me want to cut it out. Ha. Maybe I'm getting a sinus infection. Wouldn't that be splendid? Hahaha!

10/21/11 9:33 PM

I am in love with the movie *Vulgar*.

10/22/11 11:04 AM

I'm socially awkward. And, because of that, people talk down to me. Which makes me feel like tearing out their vocal chords and screaming, "just because I am a little awkward doesn't mean I'm fucking incapable of understanding when someone is being a condescending bastard!" Hmm...

10/22/11 12:13 PM

I am so fucking ugly. My skin is disgusting. I want to peel it off. Slicey dicey oh so nicely. I hate myself. Ugly. Fat. Idiotic.

Brush your hair until your scalp bleeds. Wash that skin until your face bleeds. Scrub a dub dub until there's blood in the tub.

10/22/11 2:05 PM

Depressed. Can't make up my mind about anything. Feel ugly and fat. I want to skin myself. I want to sleep forever. Let me go, world. I just want to die and jump and cut.

10/22/11 2:37 PM

Cut in the shower. Have no energy for anything. Eyelids feel heavy. Whole body is fatigued. I can barely stand writing this. I just want to sleep until I die.

I want to die.

10/22/11 4:36 PM

I don't have the motivation to clean up my own blood.

10/22/11 6:05 PM

I am forcing myself to make an entry. It is very difficult for me to focus on anything right now. I'm tired of my mood either being wonderful or terribly dreadful. And I'm tired of the most random things triggering me into a foul mood when I finally feel like I can get things done. And I just want to be as euphoric and giddy as the time I hallucinated about the monsters. But reaching that means first going through weeks or even months of pure depression and pure panic. What is going on? Perhaps it is because I never leave. And when I do leave, it is when I'm feeling at least a little functional. Up and down, in the sky, or below the ground. Never level. And if level, how long before I either sink or float again? I want to fix this (but I don't know what "this" is because I can't manage to be honest with anyone), but I am afraid that if I treat whatever this is, I will lost a significant part of myself.

Random mood swings (sometimes triggered)
Panic
OCD

Hallucinations
Anxiety
Cutting
Spending
Suicidal

Can this be fixed? Do I want it to?

10/22/11 6:34 PM
    I try to ignore this feeling, and try to act normal, but it doesn't work. I know I still come across as angry and depressed or "dramatic," and, after only a few minutes of talking, I feel like either crying, cutting, or sleeping. My body feels heavy and I can barely make it up the stairs. Let me die tonight. Please. If I wake up tomorrow, I will be surprised and angered. I am a burden on everyone, both financially and emotionally. I don't even understand what is happening, so how can I expect them to? I don't think there is anyone who genuinely likes me. I'm just an annoying, angry, reclusive girl who posts way too much online. I should die and save my family some money.

10/22/11 7:10 PM
    Hallucinations. I know I have not mentioned them much. But I will now. I remember when I was little, I would hear my favorite songs playing or marching or conversations (sounded like it was coming from outside my window). And I noticed when I'm feeling panicked, I hear and sometimes see things. I always assumed it was from a fever (although I sometimes never felt feverish). However, I am not sure where they come from.

    Why can't I ever make up my damned mind? Even the simplest of questions is hard to answer.

10/22/11 9:08 PM
    A cut a day keeps the panic at bay.

10/22/11 10:47 PM
    I have the weirdest feeling. I'm calm, yet I feel like I will die tonight. My eyes feel tired, and I just want to sleep. But I have the strangest feeling that I won't wake up. My body feels warm at the thought. And I feel exhausted. Is this fear? Or contentment? Paranoia? I guess we shall see in the morning, if I wake up.

Good-bye?

10/23/11 10:08 AM
  I woke up around 7am but was too lazy to get up. But I should have! I should have fucking gotten my ass out of bed (of course, I did my sweep of the kitchen, but I wasn't thinking). No more coffee. I should have gotten up before it was all used. I was actually feeling relaxed, minus this stupid headache and dizziness. But now I just want to cut. Let me die.
  There are blood stains on my sheets from my cuts. My room smells faintly of blood.
  Why did I not die last night? I was ready.

  Get up when you wake up.

  Skin grows back. Which means that I'll never run out of things to carve. Ha!

  There are so many pills in my room. I want to take them all. I pour them into my hands and imagine how wonderful it would feel for them to lull me to death. Oh, what is keeping me from swallowing? Bargaining with myself. But how long will I do before this silly bargaining no longer works?

10/23/11 1:20 PM
  "I have been happy, tho' [but] in a dream." –From "Dreams" by Edgar Allen Poe

10/23/11 3:49 PM
  I wrote a song.

10/23/11 4:25 PM
  I was feeling a lot better, but now I am in a terrible mood. I thought I could avoid cutting today, but I guess I can't.

  My left eye is twitching again. I hate this.

10/23/11 10:28 PM
  Cut a lot. Then ate cereal. Cereal + bloody fingers = strange taste.

  Suicidal. Thought about calling a hotline, but am too scared (yay for being terrified of making phone calls). I want to die. Die. Die. When I think about death, I either get anxiously eager or surprisingly calm (enough to put me to sleep).

I just got blood on my journal.

10/24/11 11:27 AM
So ugly. My skin is disgusting; it is majorly breaking out. I'm fat as hell. I'm covered with cuts. My hair is disgusting. My glasses are crooked and embedded themselves into my fat face. My clothes all look terrible on me. I need to clean but have no motivation. But I am going to die soon and don't want other people to have to sort through my things. My eyes/cheekbones/teeth hurt. I want to stab all and be done with it. I have so much that I should be doing, yet can't manage to leave my bed. I'm in debt. My mom has no money. And I've used up all the medical funds just so someone can tell me, "you have anxiety. Here, have some more pills." I hate that I'm causing so much financial stress, both medically and academically. I need to find a job, but am too scared that I wouldn't be able to keep it. I hate doing anything. When I'm happy, I'm too happy, and will not want to do a tiring, repetitive task– I want to run around and spin and laugh and dance. When I'm not happy, I hate everything and everyone and want to just be killed. So, in either mood, I am unproductive. But I really want to go to the clowning arts camp. But I know people think it a silly waste of money. But, if I could, I would drop everything and join the circus. Right now. I should clean. I should at least go outside. I should get over myself and this never ending anxiety, panic, and depression. I should die.

10/24/11 10:35 PM
Today was good. Terrible sinus headache, however. And terrible nausea. Contemplating majoring in Creative Writing and minoring in Art and Philosophy. Oh, and I "carved" (scratched) a pumpkin: I picked two small ones. Of course I was disappointed– my design didn't turn out as I had initially planned. Perhaps it would look better carved into my thigh! Ha! Just might do that. It can be neighbors to the three "die" marks I made last night.
Oh, I hate this head/eye/jaw/cheek pain so much.

10/26/11 2:22 PM
I haven't cut in two days! Going to work more on my *Charlotte* book.

10/30/11 7:09 PM
    I hadn't cut in several days and had been feeling okay. I went to a Halloween party last night and had a lot of fun. I was dressed as Ambassador Bennet (I feel better when I don't look like myself). Although I was stressing a lot before then– I had to get my mom to promise to pick me up when I needed to leave, regardless of the time. It was a sleepover, but I just can't do sleepovers. I can't sleep around anyone. So...I socialized a lot and met new people and slept. I woke up feeling weird. Numb (that's always bad because it means that I am on the border of something...depression, anxiety, panic, anger, happiness...I don't know). But now I feel irritated, fat, ugly, and depressed. I cut, cut, cut my left thigh. Why? Why do I feel ill after finally socializing and having fun (well, I guess I kind of know why, but still, I do not fully understand it). I just want to die. Die. Die. Die. Tomorrow is Halloween, and I do not want to spend it in some room with people who only care about food. I don't think I'm ready to go back to school. I may just die. Slicey dicey until I die.

10/30/11 7:43 PM
    I hate myself. I want to die. Life is a joke. LIFE IS A JOKE.

10/30/11 10:08 PM
    Cut again. On my upper arm/shoulder (so it can't be seen if wearing a normal short-sleeved shirt) and on my stomach– carved the word "die." I want to carve it deeper. I want that word to stay on me. Everytime I look in the mirror I will see it and it will remind me of what I want most. I suspect that cutting is what will get me through college. It is my recreational activity. It is my addiction, my beer, my cigarette. Only,

instead of damaging me on the inside, it leaves scars on the outside. Humans will just have to deal. Sure, it may lead to cutting deeper and deeper, with the possibility of causing my bleeding to death...but I don't care. After all, death is what I want most. If my cutting eventually leads to my "accidental" death, then GREAT. I'll finally have what I want.

11/1/11 11:12 AM
I hate everything. I want to die. I don't want to go back to WWC, where everyone hates me. I just want to die. I hate humans and I hate myself. Let me die.

11/3/11 2:34 PM
People ask why I'm so eager to graduate on time or early...it's because I don't expect to live very long! As if I can tell them that, though.

11/3/11 9:51 PM
I really need to die. Die die die die die.
Death.

What if I'm just heavily sedated? Then I'd still be "alive," so those people can be "happy" and I'll be in my dreams. Is the brain able to dream when in a coma? Maybe I should OD.

11/8/11 1:58 PM
I've become very bad at keeping up with my journal entries. Maybe it's because I have lost motivation to secure my thoughts. My hopes of figuring myself out are diminishing. I have been diagnosed; I know what is going on. So what is the purpose of documenting my emotions, besides the possibility that I will look back at these entries and remember the misery I felt throughout my life. Or maybe it's just because I am obsessed with remembering everything. I even find myself getting infuriated when others don't remember anything. It's offensive.

I randomly decided on the second that I will not return to Warren Wilson. I am not yet (I shall go ahead and say it) ready to leave home and therapy. It is too dangerous (as I am still quite suicidal and do not see myself working through that before January). Also, I decided that WWC is not the best fit for me. Yes, they had a circus, but I found I did not get along well with the other students (or is that me making assumptions? I confuse myself). And so I will apply to St. John's College: it seems the perfect fit— they read and write and discuss and it's quite wonderful (not that WWC doesn't do that, too...but it'd be a fresh start). Hopefully (since all the scholarships they give are need based), I will get an adequate financial aid package. This is important. Very, very important, as I will be starting as a freshman.

11/9/11 5:50 PM Depression 7/10

Depressed. Headache (terrible). Really want to cut. Haven't done anything productive, although, at least up until about a half hour ago, I was feeling okay (a bit...icky...but capable of doing more than lying in my bed, eating, drinking tea, and watching *Charmed*). Our money trouble is getting worse and worse, and although I know it is not all my fault, I still feel extremely responsible. We're in, deep (cliche statement, I know). My mom is going to sell her grand piano. Grand piano. That means everything to her. I really need to grow up and earn money so that I can help, or at least become less dependent. I feel nauseous and have a headache. I want to cut cut cut.

11/9/11 6:08 PM Depression 4/10

I cut. After not cutting since Friday (November 4th).

11/10/11 4:45 PM

I don't know how I would describe my mood for today. I've felt irritated, yet productive (well, I filled out one job app). I have felt nauseous all day, and my stomach and eyes and head hurt a lot. I am almost feeling "separate" from myself, as if I am in a haze.

Everything is making me annoyed and I really want to cut.

Someone should shoot me and stop this pressure in my head and this pain in my gut.

11/10/11 6:19 PM

Just cut with a "fresh" razor blade. My stomach is covered, but I do feel a bit better. I want to cut some more. This razor is fresh and sharp and works so well.

11/10/11 8:37 PM

Cut more on my stomach in the shower. Am drinking tea and feeling remarkably better.

Make the pain stop.

My. Head. Hurts.

11/11/11 11:38 AM

I think I am getting sick. I feel nauseous and dizzy (my balance is off). I have a horrid headache and my eyes hurt (and I am having trouble focusing). I hate feeling this way. However, although I had a strong urge to cut (and even brought my "kit" into the shower with me), I did not. This surprised me, and I wonder how long it will be until I feel the urge again.

11/13/11 8:39 PM

I had been feeling okay the past couple days (or, at least, yesterday). This morning I felt okay until about mid-day. Suddenly I felt stressed and sick. Around 4pm I was very depressed (9/10), and cut in the shower and then felt a bit better. Then I cut more and ate a ton of noodles (binge binge binge). Now I am feeling a little better, but have a terrible headache, and I can not focus my eyes. My terrible tension headaches are accompanying the sinus headaches, and my neck really hurts. Depression currently is 5/10, despite the noodles. I keep meaning to update my journal, but don't do so, usually, when feeling incapable of doing anything.

11/14/11 2:46 PM

I'm feeling okay. Not as depressed as last night, but not "happy" happy either. Is this what normality feels like? However, I have been having horrid dreams lately, and have been waking up around 3am in a panic attack (or something similar). It got me thinking though...maybe those "panic attacks" are part of my depressive episodes? Would that be why I am sometimes delusional during those (a little bit of recent reading got me thinking). It's almost as if I am paranoid! I am also wondering if these are anyway linked to the music/rambling I heard during my younger years... The faces I see on my ceiling...Spencer and Chelsea...hmmm... Anyways, I am going to see a new psychiatrist on Wednesday to start the process of finding the right "medical mix" to balance myself. I am not seeing my therapist tomorrow, so I will have to work hard to remember everything that I want to talk about– I tend to be easily distracted and go on rants that end up taking up entire sessions. On a different note, my throat seems to be swelling. I don't know if it's due to allergies, sickness, or dry skin, but it certainly does not help my anxiety level.

My throat is so annoying. It reminds me of panic.

Oh, and my headaches may be related to my TMJ problems. But I can't fix those because we're broke.

11/14/11 6:17 PM

Feeling depressed. Throat hurts. A. LOT. I want to tear it out. Don't know if sick or just anxious (about what? Hell if I know). So fuckin' what if I no longer want to eat fish?!! I need to cut. And tear this throat out, or, better yet, die.

11/15/11 10:46 AM

I have a lot of ideas and know of many things I could do, but I am also extremely irritated and so cannot successfully accomplish all of these ideas. I hate days like these. At least, when I am depressed, I don't even have motivations or ideas. But when there are ideas and you can't follow through because of random irritation and anger, it is ANNOYING.

11/15/11 11:44 AM

So many ideas. Almost annoying.

11/15/11 12:38 PM

Super energetic and excited. Dancing, have many story ideas (unfortunately can't settle down enough to work on them). Should I clean my room? Go for a walk? I would like to go to the gym, but my gym clothes expose my scars. Hmmm...

11/15/11 6:05 PM

I was going to actually do things today! I had energy and motivation and felt *gasp* optimism. Then I laid down on my bed and randomly fell asleep. Now I feel like crap.

Cut, cut.

P.S. Before I forget! I called to get "authorization" to see my new psychiatrist and was asked about my cutting. Although this question is always asked, it made me remember something that kinda bugs me: why, when I say I cut and am suicidal, do they not take me seriously? And it's not just me. People I've talked to who have similar problems don't get taken seriously until it is too late. And then they are just locked away. They're just asking for us to commit suicide (which, I guess, works out well for me).

11/16/11 1:59 PM

I am feeling okay today. My throat is acting up again, which is very annoying. I'm going to see my new psychiatrist today; I really hope he actually listens and doesn't just hear the words "anxiety, depression, and bipolar" and throw a medication at me. I want him to take time to actually know me and, by doing so, choose the best "medical mix" for this brain of mine. Oh, and I have felt a bit creative today. I have come up with some ideas for my A.I. story (which I just re-read). I'm excited for it. Although there is so much more for me to do, I think it'll turn out well. I really want to learn to animate– then I can make a short video for it. I really wish I didn't quit everything I set out to do. Maybe then I'd be able to write my own music and animate. Oh well. At least I realize how much of a failure I am.

11/16/11 2:30 PM

I'm sitting here in my mom's classroom (she has a first grade class currently). I feel panic. I think I am going to have a panic attack. I feel scared and tired and hot (sweaty) and my eyes burn and my throat is dry and everything is stuffy. I can't even go to an elementary school without having a panic attack. How will I ever get a job? Or get through college?

I really need to cut right now. I want to go home and cut. And drink peppermint tea. And then comes Jeffrey Panic.

11/19/11 7:33 PM

My new psychiatrist is nice. He actually listens. And he prescribed a drug (Lamotrigine 25mg) that seems to be working; however, there is a rare side effect which leaves me panicking all the time. Yes, I know that the chance of it affecting me is very slim, but I still freak out. And, of course, I feel the symptoms of this rare, sometimes fatal side effect (which, even after stopping the drug, can persist, get worse, and be fatal). And while the drug seems to also diminish my need to cut, when night comes along and I ponder the idea that I may suffer from this side effect, I get very panicked and the need to cut comes back. In fact, I am getting ready to cut now (although I ran out of alcohol wipes last week), and I may stop taking my meds until I see my psychiatrist on Tuesday. Ugh. I hate how illogical panic makes me. I hate, hate, hate it. The fact that I have such horrid (and stupid) anxiety and panic issues infuriates me. Time to cut. Yaaaaaaaaaaaaaay. I just hope the crash (from not taking my meds) isn't too strong. I get very suicidal when depressed (though no one ever thinks it's strange, so maybe it's really not a big deal). I tell people and they just furrow their damn eyebrows. As if that does any good to help me!!!

11/20/11 11:40 AM

Didn't take my meds (for Bipolar) last night. Still feeling a bit paranoid; I hate, hate, hate this.

11/21/11 8:37 PM

Panic attack. I feel as if my skin is going to peel and boil off of my bones. I'm so itchy and my throat is dry. And I just want to tear my body up myself. At least then I'd be in control. Must change sheets. Itchy. Itchy. Itchy. Can't breathe and can't think. I don't want the faces to come back like the last time I felt like this. I hate this!

11/22/11 4:45 PM

Felt really depressed this morning, and really didn't feel like seeing psychiatrist (they just never listen!). But being with two cute dogs (petsitting) made me feel a lot better. Suddenly feel creative.

P.S. Still scared to take bipolar meds.

11/27/11 12:20 PM

Been panicking a lot. Also been thinking a lot about Ambassador Bennet. Not really sure why.

Emily Carol was an introverted child. However, she enjoyed being around people, and had quite the imagination. As she grew older, the other children became almost offended by her odd "darkness." And eventually, as she became a preteen, she was rejected and her sense of self split apart. Emily (sad, lonely, and passive, lived within her own mind, hoping to join her imaginary friends in the unreal worlds). She felt there were many parts of herself: there was Carol (rebellious and outspoken), Charlotte (the child with a beautiful imagination, yet some doubt), Max (trapped in her reflection, sort of a sociopath), Ruth (the psychopath), Andrew (the energetic and creative boy), and so many others. Then there was Ambassador Benedict Bennet: someone whom Emily truly wanted to be; ABB has no gender, and is a blend of all of Emily's "personalities." Oh, how she longed to be Ambassador Bennet. As Emily suffered through depression, bullying, hate, judgment, anxiety, panic, and bipolar disorder, her suicidal thoughts became stronger, and she attempted suicide, was discovered, and entered into a coma (caused from her drug overdose). As this happened, however, she woke up within her own world (in her head) and was surrounded by all of her personalities. Emily became ABB, joined her clown friend, Michael (Mr. Clown), and became a dimension hopping space pirate surfing through imagination and wonder.

11/27/11 2:40 PM
      Heart beating– can feel throughout body. And my arms are
twitching, as if I have no control. Am extremely irritated and need to cut
cut cut cut cut!

      People tell me to stop stressing as if I can fucking control that.
"It's just a thought. It's not true. So calm down." Ha! If thinking like that
solved such problems, then I wouldn't have to be in therapy in the first
place, now would I. This heart pounds and I feel it all through my body.
My insides hurt. My arms twitch. My throat is sore and dry. I can't eat
anything without feeling sick or disgustingly fat. And I slice my skin and
make a mess, only to realize I am out of alcohol wipes, which makes me
panic and want to cut more. Oh yes, it is so easy for me to fix this. So. easy.
So mock me when I get scared or angry, or tell me to not overthink or
worry about things. 'Cause that'll surely do a lot of good. IDIOTS. Just let
me fucking kill myself. Then you won't have to deal with my annoying
tendencies. And maybe I'll finally be happy. When they say, "it gets
better...," that's complete bullshit. It may get tolerable for a week or so,
maybe a few months, a year, years. And then it comes crashing down and
makes you feel worse than ever before. These voices, like someone is
blowing, making a "whoosh" noise in my ear, right as I gasp and my arms
twitch and I continue to panic, because that's what I have been told to do.
Take pills and wait until it goes away. Well, it will NEVER GO AWAY.

11/28/11 6:41 PM
      Annoyed with myself. Everything I do and every response I get
makes me want to die or cut. And I am sick of people claiming I am just
being "dramatic." Yeah, that's why I, who has tried to stay ahead, is now
falling behind and taking time off of school. And I'm sick of being scolded
for not taking my meds: I won't take pills that make me panic. And my gut
hurts. It feels like someone poured acid in my intestines. My heart
pounds. I'm fat and ugly. I cut both yesterday and today, and will cut just
as soon as I am finished writing this.

"A Hesitance to Medicate" by Emily Carol

You claim this anger puts me in danger
Decided that my life needs to be in safer hands
Your books have taught you, from all their experiences
A myriad of methods you don't even understand

47

Do you even have a clue
What your judgment puts me through?
Would you follow as they instruct you to
If the subject were not me but you?

You say I should amend
These thoughts that never end
Does your solution require more rituals
On which I must depend?
Why don't you explain again
How my life will not truly begin
Until I've deserted all I've learned to love
Deserted how I've learned to live

You ask to understand
So you can fix me
You ask to understand
So you can fix me?

How can I ever possibly find
A way to describe these worlds in my mind
Especially to the blind
To those who will never realize:
Real or imagined?
Both are bound to happen
Although they may seem as delusions, twinkling illusions
They're real to those who can see
Without them we could not be
They are our reality
Yet you dare to ask this of me?

You preach that, in time, with your professional guidance
My mind will clear and become a safer tool
These thoughts shall slow; I'll sleep peacefully at night
I can trade my wonder to become a blissful fool

Do you even have a clue
What your judgment puts me through?
Would you follow as they instruct you to
If the subject were not me but you?

I can see how you would think
How it shouldn't be so hard to choose
That I might as well put these to use
Rather than suffer from my own abuse
But after years of this devotion
To my mind's erratic emotions
I do fear that this practical plan
Will erase part of who I am

How can I ever possibly find
A way to describe these worlds in my mind
Especially to the blind
To those who will never realize:
Real or imagined?
Both are bound to happen
Although they may seem as delusions, twinkling illusions
They're real to those who can see
Without them we could not be
They are our reality
Yet you dare to ask this of me?

You ask to understand
So you can fix me
You say you understand
And that you can fix me
You ask to understand
So you can fix me
You say you understand
And that you can fix me?
By hiding away what makes me?
By stealing the pain that saves me?

How can I ever possibly find
A way to describe these worlds in my mind
Especially to the blind
To those who will never realize:
Real or imagined?
Both are bound to happen
Although they may seem as delusions, twinkling illusions
They're real to those who can see
Without them we could not be

They are our reality
Yet you dare to ask this of me?

Should I lean over and allow a ladder to uncurl from my mind
To guide you into this reality of mine
Where my enemies and friends reside
And from your treatment hide?

12/4/11

The only reason I haven't killed myself is because my family would have no way to pay for my funeral. The moment I feel they're a bit financially stable, I'M GONE.

12/5/11 9:05 PM

I need to die.

12/6/11

I want to swallow all of my pills and then slit my wrists. I'm just a leech. I need to die.

12/6/11 8:10 PM

Things that make me anxious:
- Eating in front of people
- Being in crowds
- Eating
- Taking meds with bad side effects
- Fire
- Not knowing if house is "secure" (fire)
- Drawing, reading, writing, working on anything in front of people
- Noises that cause me to not be able to get to and maintain sleep

12/8/11

I called a hotline and they told me that they'd call me back. If that's not a sign...

Fuck them ALL.

Magickal Morose's Miscellaneous Musings

April 2009 (Dreams)
A murderer was on the loose, and I ran to an empty house (mansion really) and realized that when someone is killed, their spirit goes to live in the mansion. After learning this, I told him to kill me so I could hang out with my friends. But he said no.

When I was young (Dreams)
- There was a set on stage that looked like a room in a large mansion. If you walked into it, it changed from a set to a real mansion. The other kids in the play and I would play around in it, but if we went into the upstairs bathroom, the spirits in them would trade places and take over our bodies. I freaked out because I had to find a way to switch it back to normal by opening night.

- TRICKIES! German Castle Haunting

Some time in April 2009 (Dream)
We were playing hide and seek in the dark in a mansion. To hide, everyone lay down on the ground and I kept falling over them. There was a large saint bernard sleeping by a window. I pet him.

5/9/2009 - 5/10/2009 (Dream)
I had the flu and fell out of my chair in advisory and died. My friend looked down at me, stood up, scooted her chair away, and sat back down.

5/27/2009 (Dream)
We (GSA club) were in a large store and had to put on a good performance or we'd be killed by these soldier-things. One of the members had to escape home to get a backing track, so he climbed through the air vents while we all distracted our enemies. Luckily, he returned with the track, and we performed Buffy's "I'll never Tell."

5/30/2009 (Dreams)
My math teacher was angry because I needed to take a test, but I had to move to a different location to take it. Unfortunately, the mist from Stephen King's The Mist was rolling over my school, so it was hard to find a place where I could see what I was doing, so my teacher led me to a tent and told me to work right outside it but not go in. As I was taking my test,

two people came and pulled me into the tent with them. Once in, the time shifted and we were in our bodies of our past lives and had to relive when we all killed each other. Then, as dead bodies, we stood up and embraced each other (we forgave each other) and then we dissolved (?) and I was back, lying inside an empty tent, and with an incomplete math test. My teacher was angry and failed me, then sent me to the *Animal Farm*, where I was lectured by Napoleon and then chased out of the farm by him and his followers.
...ODD...

"I'm gonna pull your nails out
I'm gonna hear you scream and shout
But no one help will be around
To—"

6/28/2009 - 6/29/2009 (Dream)
     My family was in Virginia. One day, A took us three kids somewhere, used poor driving skills, and the car ended up flipping over around 7 times. I was a little annoyed. The next day, instead of doing the same as the previous day, I convinced my mom to let us take a little trip to Connecticut (then I could visit C). My mom agreed to drive, and I took forever to pack. My grandpa was angry that we were going to Connecticut. I remember all the good things that happened, including the strange dance with clothes everywhere. Just as I'm about to enter the car, I wake up...still in Fresno.

8/7/2009-8/8/2009 (Dream)
     I went to Hollins University for college, along with a few other CW kids. One of my professors seemed to like me and bought me gifts and finished some of my homework essays. Me and my friends talked about how fun college was and how free and independent we all felt. One evening, my friends and I were sitting outside a movie theatre when security guards ran after some man (the teacher?). While the guards were distracted, we snuck into the movies.

8/10/2009-8/11/2009 (Dream)
     L, C, and I were thinking of walking to Japan Town while mom was gone. But somehow she was still able to give us a ride. On the way there we met Grandma and Grandpa who were very disappointed that we were spending money. We parked and continued our journey. We walked

around and looked at shops (I liked some odd pins). One shop owner pushed me down a ramp.

8/11/2009-8/12/2009 (Dream)
School started and my teachers (a brother and sister) were really "right-brained". The gal taught me math and science through singing and the guy would use skits and art. Our classroom was a really pretty and "woodsy" backyard, and we students sat on the swings during lessons.

8/20/2009-8/21/2009 (Dream)
I was adopted by a couple and their friend. We moved to a strange remote area with deserted woods and hills and ruins. I notice they are hiding something from me, and I begin a plan to escape. At one point I was taking a bath and the lady got pissed because I used her husband's face wash. That night I escaped into the woods. I raced up grassy hills and hid in the grass.

8/19/2009-8/20/2009 (Dream)
A girl pulled me down a long sidewalk surrounded by pretty gardens and through a door. We stood on a large hill. She spread her arms and said, "Isn't this magnificent?"

8/23/2009-8/24/2009 (Dream)
We moved to a haunted house (the ghosts were from *The Devil's Rejects*) and I became good friends with them. One morning, I woke up sick. Everything was spinning. My mom claimed that the ghosts had infected me. She took me to the emergency room, and I worried about missing CART (which, in this dream, was just a cafeteria where we did long packets). While in the waiting room, an elderly lady dressed in Hollins clothes knocks on the window, and someone lets her in. She is apparently a Hollins alumnae who wanted to speak with me. Later, when I go back to CART, the teacher seems very angry and gives me a lot of packets to do. [Very unlike CART.]

9/6/2009-9/7/2009 (Dream)
We moved to a town we hadn't been in since we were young and opened a clothing shop.

4/21/2010-4/22/2010

I dreamed of a *Mulan* song. When I went on Facebook, I noticed one of my friends had the song as her status. I also dreamed that my grandpa accepted gays.

There are so many cool worlds inside my mind. I wonder if they are real...

Mid July 2010 (Dreams)

There was a strange cave in an amusement park and me and several other people fell in. It was a strange land and there were many strange creatures. In order to survive, we had to find "The Fruit Punch." We managed to escape, but another guy and I returned to explore. I got sick, but we found "The Fruit Punch" in time.

I visited C in Connecticut, and her house was a maze.

There was a strange world where roller coasters were used as buses. The surrounding planets had the same plans (you could see the tracks on their surfaces). Lovers kept trying to kill each other. There was a strange closed off pond in the ocean which had ground filters that sucked you down unless you were in a boat. I kept having flashbacks about those. There was a woman who was obsessed with being precise.

Balcony overlooks the sea. Strange girl with black and purple hair is always there.

July 2010 (Dream)

Strange king and queen (siblings?) who each own half of a land. The king causes pain but keeps control, and the queen seems to have disappeared, but her half is doing fine. The king slowly uses magic to spread death and darkness throughout the queen's land. A girl (me, I think) was asleep on the edge of the queen's half and woke up surrounded by weird ash and dead plants.

10/7/2010-10/8/2010 (Dream)

I had a dream in the form of a musical. There was a crew on a spaceship; they were singing. On Earth, a boy dreams of something more (and hides in lamps). The girl on the ship notices the boy and sends a double helix ladder down to earth, through the roof and onto the kitchen table. He joins her after she explains that he does not belong on Earth.

They climb the double helix ladder and onto the spaceship. The ladder expanded and then disappeared.

4/4/2012
It has been nearly four months since I made a journal entry. I just couldn't bring myself to write in that journal full of anger and depression. I mean, it actually has blood in it. I felt that I needed a new journal– one that is not tainted, but balanced and free. Honestly, I have wanted this particular journal for several years, so I was so delighted to finally be able to buy it. I love it, and am so excited to see how many ideas and stories and magic it will come to hold. I'll be honest: not everything in here will be chipper and diddle-dandy; that would be impossible. But it will definitely hold a new perspective.

4/9/2012
I'm going to try to focus on making myself more sensitive to my surroundings. I would love to be more attached to the paranormal world– I think I'd make great friends, and have always been in love with the paranormal, and have had some experiences of my own.

5/29/2012
I apologize for not writing as much. I used to write several times a day; however, that was all fueled by pain and anger. I guess I ought to write more about the positive things, and about my thoughts on certain ideas or topics. Perhaps, journal, I shall give you a name... I shall let you know once I think of one.
I really ought to start eating healthier! Hopefully, I wish...wish to have SMALLER BOOBS.

6/14/2012
I am becoming even more concerned about my medications. I am having depressive days similar to those that I had before I was medicated. I am afraid that I am regressing. I am afraid to stay alone in my room. I want to have social interaction, but I fear no one likes me. My brain is beginning to trick me again. It is good that I am aware that it is not displaying total reality, but it still makes me feel like shit. I want help, but I don't know where to get it. I already have a psychiatrist and a therapist. Who else could help?

6/19/2012

I feel like I am going to have a panic attack. I feel so warm, but I'm not sweating. I took some Xanax, but it doesn't feel like it is working. I really worry about my meds, and I am questioning whether or not I should go back to the mental health center. But I don't feel like it would be good to start new meds two months before I leave for school only to have another mental breakdown. But my depression is coming back worse and worse. The need to cut is coming back as well. Why the fuck is this happening?!! Everything seemed to be going so well...and now everything is shit. I don't know what to do. My anxiety level has increased so much. SO MUCH. I don't want to regress. I don't want my cycles to become so extreme again. I don't want to give into this strong urge to cut. Everytime– every minute, I feel the urge to cut. I don't know what I should do. What should I do? What should I FUCKING DO?!! I hate this. And I hate that the monster side of me is taking over again. I thought I had killed it. But it's back. They're all back. They are back and they want me to cut and cut and cut until I feel so miserable that I need to cut myself until I slice all of the life out of me. It's amusing really...how easily the urge to die comes back. What happened to the balance? I had finally found balance, and then it was gone. I want the fucking balance back.

6/19/2012

I feel like the energy has been stolen away from me. I'm sitting here, waiting for my therapist appointment. All I want to do is curl up with a blanket, cut, and cry. But is there any reason? No. It's just some stupid trick that my brain is playing on me. It's almost as if it enjoys being so chemically imbalanced. I guess I had put too much trust in myself and my meds– I thought I had finally become stronger than my disorders. I was wrong. So very, very wrong. I feel my brain laughing (or rather, the disorders laughing). They are probably amused by my frustration. "Ha! She really thought those stupid meds would keep us quiet? What an idiot. We won't stop. We can never, EVER be stopped. Even when she kills herself, we will still be here laughing." They are no longer silent, you see. They are loud. And none of their intentions are kind. I had thought that my family would understand, but they think I am just being a bitch, now that I'm medicated, apparently ALL my symptoms should have disappeared, right? Is that what they all think? My meds made everything lighter, and helped me stabilize, but I still experience my symptoms. A few pills won't get rid of a disorder that will forever be with me.

6/20/2012

     Waiting to be checked into the behavioral health center once again. Good-bye piercings. Although, I guess it's better to swap piercings for sanity. But it's still hard. My face feels naked. I haven't been admitted and I already feel like I'm in a kindergarten class. Just because we have psychological issues DOES NOT mean that we are not capable of adult conversation. In fact, the condescension that takes place here was the main reason I left...I hate the fakeness (is that even a word?) of some of the employees. I'm a fucking adult. Treat me like one. I know they have all the power, but I would appreciate it if they would talk to us as their equals, not their pre-school students. Ugh. My therapist told my mom I was displaying "psychotic mania." Irrational. Angry. Cynical. Unsure. Torn. Aggravated. When I am like that, there is no logic anywhere inside me. It's as if I take something small (and even nothing at all) and exaggerate and become paranoid and judgemental— which has caused many of my acquaintances to hate me. It caused me to hate myself. I was blowing everything out of proportion...and reading things wrong– I was sure everyone hated me– and I became angry. I walk by people and think of them all as disgusting idiots who judge me and heckle me for no reason. I have recently learned that this is a symptom of "psychotic mania." If I do get admitted, I will definitely make it known that I will not put up with this "kindergarten" treatment. I will let them know when I feel offended. It's a bitchy thing to do, but, right now, they are adults– we should be able to handle honesty.

     I know my ranting makes me sound like a non-appreciative person. However, I honestly do appreciate the nice, clean, and efficient atmosphere here. It's much better than some of the health centers/wards that I have read about. And I like how they cater to my dietary needs.

     I'm hungry.

     Oh, I really hope I get into Unit 2 at least sometime today... I understand that the people in the other units mean no harm, but the treatment there is so much less beneficial to me than the treatment in Unit 2. Also, some of those patients are quite stinky. Interesting, but stinky. Let's hope that this stay will put me back on my feet for good.

     We shall see.

6/20/2012

     So, after hours of waiting, I finally got settled. And, although they have no rooms in Unit 2 available right now, they are letting me stay here until a bed opens up. Yah! Whoo! I think it's interesting, however... they don't allow pens, but they allow pencils. Pencils are much more dangerous.

I am also fascinated by the fact that they did not make me remove my piercings... this made me outrageously happy... my face feels so naked without them. So, I guess, things are good. My therapist will be pleased that I finally did as she asked. HA! Let's hope I finally get my meds straightened out before I leave for school (which will be in less than two months).

Apparently my shorts were too short.

They noticed my piercings, but they haven't made me remove them. I hope their generosity will last the duration of my stay. And I am not looking forward to the inevitable caffeine withdrawal. So far, the people I've met here are very kind.

My experience this time is MUCH, MUCH better than the last two. I suspect that part of it is that I'm partially medicated and less lost in a thick fog. I still find that people (the staff) tend to talk down to us, but I will forgive them...for now.

I want to sleep. But my hair is wet.

I think it is amusing that they allow us to watch violent movies in the day room. It's still going pretty well. It annoys me, however, that the unit's activities go pretty late into the night. I'd think that they'd want to make sure that we'd get adequate sleep. Maybe I will ask for them to give me a sleep aid, just in case.

It's time for the nightly check-in. I often wonder what the nurses truly think of us. I understand that some of them enjoy it– I mean, they chose the career. But I wonder if they think we are so weak and inferior. I know they mean well, but I feel as if they treat us like children. I want to be spoken to as an equal. I have to keep myself from responding sarcastically or making snarky comments when they talk to us like that. I am miffed at how I wasn't able to meet with my psychiatrist. That was the reason that I came here– my therapist wanted me safe until I was prescribed more meds (or replaced my current meds). I'm hoping that I see him early tomorrow. I know my therapist and my mom want me to stay longer this time, but I find that I do better when I make my own schedule. And I miss my cats. And my clown. It doesn't take long for me to become impatient while in inpatient care. Ha.

6/21/2012

Ah. I have such a horrible headache. I need coffee, but they only have decaf.

I really am not looking forward to the 45 minutes we have to spend in the gym (which is horribly cold). I doubt anyone in my unit will want to play some jolly game of basketball, or go on one of the exercise machines. We're depressed! And fucking anxious. Yet we are still aware. It seems silly to prance around a gym at a mental health center. I figure the patients in the other units have more fun because they really aren't too aware of themselves or where they are.

Why does it take so long to see the fucking doctor?!!

It's amusing that this place goes through a lot to make sure everyone is safe. However, there are so many ways for people to harm themselves here. Do they assume that since we are ill, we cannot put two and two together? I mean, really. They don't allow pens, but they allow pencils? Pencils are much easier to use to kill or cut oneself. And there are so many other "risks" as well:

- Pencils
- Pillows
- Trash bags
- Heavy doors
- Sinks
- Pants (can hang around neck)
- The poorly supervised pool

I haven't been able to see my psychiatrist yet!!! If it takes too long, then it will be too late for me to be discharged tonight. And I don't think I could stand another day here. I don't eat certain types of food, so they assume that I have eating problems. They even had a nurse test me to see if I may have an eating disorder. Idiots! I know that, medically, they know what they are doing, but I don't think they trust or think highly of us. I don't want the stupid activity groups with stupid games and cheesy lessons. If I'm here, I want good therapy and doctor visits. That's it! If they add anymore of this pre-school hosh-posh, then I will go crazy(er). I'm tired. I'm annoyed. Fuck. I just want to see the fucking psychiatrist and case manager.

6/29/2012

I feel nauseous. I keep getting fucking manhandled. Gross men with their wandering hands and wet, unwanted kisses. I know that I should help with the flyer routes, but I feel so incredibly sick by what happened yesterday.

On another note, I had quite the interesting dream last night:

I had a roommate who was sad because her ex-boyfriend couldn't get over the death of his younger brother (who was decapitated by a motorcycle during an indoor chase in the dorm common room). Every afternoon/night, the ex-boyfriend goes to his brother's grave (he was buried in the school cemetery). Every night, a green light/fog comes from a nearby hill. He follows it, but it disappears once he gets close to it. The girl tries to get him to start moving on, but he gets annoyed with her. She gives me a vase that his brother gave her the day before he died. She wanted me to return it to him. I was unsure, since he was irritable. I started on my way to the cemetery, but got lost in a green fog. I heard someone saying that if I pass a test (and win) I will get the ex-boyfriend's brother's soul back, which, once above ground, would bring him back to life. I was told to bring the vase with me. A door appeared in the ground, and it opened and I went down a stairway. There was a long hallway— I walked until I found a doorman standing next to a cabinet. Another girl appeared, claiming to want the same thing— she was unnaturally infatuated with the dead brother, but, since she was not human, she would take his soul away from the human world. We were to go through a "magic" obstacle course, which had hidden paths and staircases and traps (we had to find the right way— even if it meant jumping into a hole under a couch). We were told to meet at a specific location before the "green man" came. I was far behind the other girl, but met at the location. The green man appeared and was quite cunning. He claimed that he would be joining the "tournament." He collected coveted souls to keep him alive. He was actually quite friendly. I'm not exactly sure what happened during the final part of the "race" thing, but the green man got the vase (which everyone kept trying to get from me the entire time). He jumped onto a platform and held up the vase which emitted a green light and a floating green bracelet. A whirling hole opened up and pushed wind down on the girl and me. The girl fell after only moments of magically hovering. I jumped onto the platform as it rose high in the sky. The wind was pushing down hard on me, and the hole in the "roof" was getting wider, and the bracelet was getting brighter. I climbed onto the platform, tried to grab the vase, but was blown down by the wind. I held onto the platform, demanding that I get the vase because too many people were in pain. I couldn't hold on, and, as I fell, the green man used one hand to keep me from falling. The vase was still in his other hand. After a while, I began to slip, and he dropped the vase (which shattered) and pulled me up. He put the glowing green bracelet around my wrist (the bracelet being what held the boy's soul). I had fought the hardest. The green man disappeared after helping me back to the surface.

12/9/2012

It has been exactly one year since I last cut. Whooo! I'd celebrate, but I have so much to do. Oh well. I got some free tea, so I'll take that as an anniversary gift.

Dream: Beach Dream/reality: weird restaurant in the hills of a beach town...with access to other dimensions/realities/etc... (scenery reminded me of Pismo). I lived in a wooden estate nearby with some ghosts and worked at an adult store.

12/16/14

"You came out of a stained glass window. Essentially could have shattered you and made all your bits all pokey and abstract– stuck you together with spit. I've always wanted to dive through a window, head first, you know, but I gave that up for you. I helped you out of that prison politely and held your hand and made sure you weren't hurt in the process. So don't complain to me and put me down or I will shove you, impolitely, and not elegantly, back in that window, dive through it head first, and scatter you around junkyards all over the state. You'll never get put back together, you thick egg, and you'll just watch the clouds."

Magickal Morose: The Melancholy Always Finds Me

5/7/2016

   I am now living in Arroyo Grande— just a few minutes away from Pismo. I work at a bakery. It's weird that Sunkist's passing brought me here. Midnight came with me, of course. It is Saturday, my day off. I am sitting on a bench at the park. A seagull is stalking me. Ha! He wants my crumb roll, I suppose.

5/9/2016

   I don't know what I'm doing here. I have fallen upon bad habits. I've had them, but I don't have to hide them. I know I am an alcoholic, and I won't deny that I adore my occasional cigarette. I am fascinated by the sea, and can stare into it for a long time before realizing how much time has passed. Cliche, I know. I am happy here, but am also depressed. I can't cry, but I feel I want to all the time. I laugh so much when I am in the ocean. I feel as if I am so happy. I have never felt such a feeling except when I am in the sea. I'm not sure why, as I grew up in a bullshit desert. I want to accomplish something with my writing. I want to be someone more than the average person I am. It breaks me. I want to be important. I've left all my loved ones behind and so this is my last chance.
   I'll write more soon.

5/29/2016

   Writer's block is the best. Especially when the ideas are releasing so much adrenaline, but I have no idea how to put them into words/organize them/get started.
   FRUSTRATED.

6/16/2016

   I slept a lot yesterday. Probably got at least twelve hours before going into work this morning. And, of course, I had a myriad of vibrant dreams, of which I remember very little. I pieced together some bits throughout the day. I will rewrite what I wrote, and will add whatever else may return to my mind as I record the notes:
   Not noted in order
   I was preparing for a costume party, and was going to be associating with a group of girls from my elementary school, but at our present ages (mine is 23 currently). However, there was a lot of deceit occurring and all were against me, and I knew/found out that they were planning some intense "revenge," or the likes, against me on the night of

the party. I, in turn, was also planning something (which I don't remember...) which would lead to their misfortune once carried out. The setting was in a hotel/dorm. I often dream of buildings in this style, and I always seem to jump/float up and down the staircases, and they usually have strange, somewhat dangerous elevators.

The bathrooms/showers in this building were nasty– many of the doors could not lock, close, were see-through, were simply tarps, etc... and most stalls and showers were taken. The ones left were not private enough for my taste. I was trying my best to get ready, but I could not find a proper area to shower/change/use the restroom (I think I was on my period). I don't remember what my initial costume was going to be. I had announced it to my friends who would be visiting me for the party that evening (JC, DA, and MJ– MJ attended the same "school" as me and also lived in the building). The morning of the costume party, about an hour before we had "classes," MJ and I were driving back to the building/school and I was entertaining the idea of changing my costume. I thought it'd be nice to dress as Leeloo from *The Fifth Element* (I planned on doing a crummy version, but I knew/figured the other attendees would know who I was. I also knew not all of them would have superb costumes).

MJ mentioned that we had time to possibly go to a Target. I thought it was a good idea. For some reason we didn't go, and I found out my friend had some clothes I may be able to borrow– I also thought I'd check the "free piles" in the building. (The friend I just mentioned is MB, whom I met in the eighth grade.) She ended up not having the right clothes for Leeloo, and, if she did, I did not want to cut them up, which I would have had to do. I dropped the idea of the Leeloo costume, although MJ and MB did mention one final time that we could go to Target if I really wanted to. I declined. I decided I would go as a make-shift Joker. I'm not sure all that was going on, but I knew I had ulterior motives for the majority of what I was doing at the party. "The Group," as I will call them, had something bad planned for me, and I managed to find it out. I then told a couple of them to be aware that I had something planned for them as well. Again, I have no idea what my plan was, nor if I had, overall, good intentions. I only know that, as I revealed myself to having also been deceptive, it was admitted as a warning. I felt bad. Guilty. In a way, I was trying to help them. Perhaps make them avoid doing/going to what it was that I needed them to do and where I wanted them to go. I began to get dressed, and went from a "Joker" theme to a "witch" theme. I will draw what I can gather that I looked like outfit-wise (I remember being quite upset that I did not have a witch hat).

In another one of my dreams, I was visited by my dear cat, Sunkist. I must mention that, whenever she appears in my dreams, I know she is not real. I know she is dead. And I know that I am dreaming. I always try to make her presence last as long as possible, and I force myself to perceive more "sensory details." I can feel her and hear her, and she is, perhaps, as real as a dream can make her. She is warm and soft, and her loud, vibrating purr is exactly as it was when she was alive. She is on a cat tree, and I am thrilled. She, as always, fades not long after I walk to/embrace her– her deed of greeting and of comforting is done. Bandit also appears in my dreams occasionally, although he is less "real" than Sunkist in regards to my perception of him– I do not *feel* him as I do her. Eliza, in this dream, kept escaping from my room. For some reason, my door in my dream (in the AG condo) was a sliding door which failed to close all the way. I tried to block it, but kept, stupidly, using lightweight items such as cereal boxes. This is frustrating, and I am glad that my other cat, Midnight, does not try to leave my room, but only watches as Eliza escapes (Eliza, in waking hours, is staying with Midnight and me, and has been "asking" to leave the room a lot. Loudly. Early in the morning. While I'm trying to get in my last few hours of sleep before work at 6am). I do not know if I ended up "fixing" the door.

But back to the party mentioned earlier on: I made my entrance as a "witch" with no hat, and I was no longer wearing my bolero/shawl. For some reason, I also feel that I was barefoot. Honestly, I am very foggy as to how this scene ended. I know I spotted my visitor friends while I was out of costume and "pouncing" back and forth around the building and up and down the stairs– in my mind, I knew they were dressed up, although they appeared to be in normal clothes...I felt bad for having not decided on a costume yet. But entering the costume party as a hatless, barefoot witch is how I remember that segment/theme of the dream ending...!

The notes I recorded at work included one more brief part of my dreams, but I cannot figure out what it was! The pen was drying out/not on a good surface, and only a few letters from each word made it onto the paper. Hopefully I'll be able to decipher it in time. Ha!

6/17/2016

I am very upset. I feel as if I have no place– as cliche as it is. Of course, part of me does not care what other people think. What did I do? I know that I irritate some of my co-workers, but I do feel I can rectify that over time. I'm now looking for rooms on craigslist. At least I know my budget and what I can get by with paying for on this job's paycheck. Besides, perhaps a better living environment would be beneficial. I don't really enjoy the atmosphere of the condo. Perhaps I am only trying to convince myself, though, to reduce the anxiety that comes from being unwanted and thought of as a horrid roommate.

6/19/2016
   I love my Betsey Johnson pen.

6/22/2016 (Dream)
   Grandparents house with an extra bedroom from dead "sister" and back "doors" (giant) that lead to the inside of a chapel.
   In my recent dream in this location, I inquired with new owners on whether or not they had discovered the "chapel" thing which never had more than a dozen people in it regardless of its massive size.

6/23/2016
   Gonna be short on rent for July. I fail. So here I am— at the bar.

6/29/2016
   I am displeased with myself in many ways, but, mostly, for now, I am displeased by my lack of control over my finances. I think I'm going to get better, but I just get worse. And, oh! Guess where I am sitting now, as my bank account is low and I need to borrow money tomorrow, so as not to be short of my rent? I'm at the bar! I love it here, but it just proves my lack of control over myself. At least I binge-watched *American Mary*, its featurettes, and the commentary, as well as got some art done...all after missing work because of my anxiety and the drinking that kills my stomach lining (and I'm sure my liver is not the happiest organ right now, either).
   I really need to start working on my funhouse idea, besides just jotting down the same notes periodically through the week. I'm so excited with all I can do with it, but still feel discouraged and mediocre and just...below average. And when it comes to my art, I feel like moist garbage. I NEED to take art classes. I'm trash! I just draw variations of the same thing. When it comes to my writing and drawing "progress" I find that there is none. I feel like Kiki when she loses her powers (oh, and that DVD got stuck after she sees the bread design, and won't play beyond. TYPICAL).

Depressed
And
Stressed

And
Always letting
People down...

6/29/2016

I know I wrote down brief notes about the following dream somewhere, but as I have most of it fresh in my mind, I feel that I should re-record what I remember in case it never comes back to me or I cannot find the paper on which I previously recorded the dream: (It will be spotty, and so I'll try to find the original paper with the dream).

I was in some sort of mental hospital (I was on floor 1) that appeared to have once been a theatre. We would have group therapy on the stage; there were only a dozen or so people on my floor.

(Will continue this entry later. I am anxious, depressed, and can't focus right now.)

Notes on above dreams from 4-3-2016

MJ was a psychiatrist at a mental hospital I was staying at. I was on floor 1, and she was transferred to work on floor 3. I ask to go see what floor 3 looks like. She cannot let me, due to "house rules." Eventually, she shows me her office. Each doc has an "elevator-type" office that moves from floor to floor. It's cool. I couldn't go out to the 3rd floor. Apparently the 3rd floor is super crowded with "over 60 people," MJ says. I believe floor 1 only has 13-15?

At the very end, I had some sort of psychiatric breakdown and announced it to the lady in charge of floor 1. (Oh, our floor area looked like a stage and theater). She took me out of our "area" and set me on the floor against a wall while she did something in an office. Down the hall was a huge open area with hospital cot things and people with IVs in their arms. They looked oddly content, and there was a huge skylight.

7/2/2016

Painted a lot today. A bit.

7/3/2016

I
LOVE GHOSTS
I
LOVE ALL THINGS
PARANORMAL

7/3/2016

Last night I was quite upset about how on Friday, the ghost residing in my coworker's grandparents' home ignored me, even though I very strongly wished to communicate with him. I really was on the verge of tears (!).

In my dream, I lived in a haunted home. I was renting the room; I do not know who all else lived there. There were familiar faces from my waking life, but I do not recall whom they belonged to. I was trying to communicate with the spirit, who manifested the most in my bedroom, since I was the most open to him– everyone else was terrified of him. I was very upset, for I felt that he felt the same about me. I was never fearful of him. One night (not sure if I was dreaming or awake...I am leaning towards it being in a dream, for the setting seemed to change to an abandoned dining room type place, with old furniture and a wall lined with windows. It was a very comfortable room), I knew the ghost was there, and I called out and willed him to me (he needed help coming closer and manifesting into a person I could actually see).

I felt him coming closer and saw a brief outline fluctuation/difference in the light surrounding his spirit. I was very emotional and happy to finally be so close (and I could tell that he, once again, felt the same). I grabbed what I knew was the location of where his hand would be, and as I did so, I willed more energy towards him and he appeared almost wholly human (still a little "floaty" and a bit transparent). His hand was in mine, and we both were happy. It was overwhelming how warm we both felt finally being together. He felt more solid and human and we hugged tightly. We conversed and were great friends. It felt like love to me, which is fascinating. I don't remember all the details of what all else occurred, as there was chaos in the home I lived in in my dream. But I felt closer to and could communicate better with the ghost during my waking hours (in my dream still, not in real life where I am writing this).

I wish I knew more details. Perhaps they'll come back to me. (He had a very simple name, like Billy or Jim or something like that.)

7/22/2016

I've missed an entire week of work, and already am having shit luck in regards to my financial situation. On meds for the stupid sinus infection that caused this mess. Of course, part of that treatment was a fucking steroid shot, and I think it heightened my depression. I understand, from what the doctors have accounted, that if it is to have side effects, it will cause a manic episode. However, upon reading online, I've found several claims that the shot could indeed cause a depressive episode, especially in psychiatric patients. I was already upset and depressed, but now I feel like I did in 2011 when I was on no meds at all. Maybe it nullifies my psych meds? I have no idea. But, currently, I feel disgusting, stupid, fat, lazy, irresponsible, unaccomplished, tired, etc...with $9 to my name.

7/29/2016

Dream: I was writing a novel, but as I read through it, I was living it. (Ghost story: violent and eerie...both typical and fascinating for me.) Three(?) ghosts who eventually learned how to look solid.

7/31/2016

I'm going to do my best to remember my dream which I plan to take notes on on Friday (it is the yellow paper to the left). It may take a few visits to this page to get a good amount of details recorded.

8/15/2016

Got hit with some horrid depression. Planned some steps that will hopefully help– I hope I don't end up disappointing people too much. Missed a full day of work today. I am a loser.

My body issues are getting strong again and are starting to consume my mind again.

8/21/2016

In a recent dream, someone led me away from the group/city I was with/in and made me pretend that I wanted to go, and had their arm wrapped around my shoulders as we walked.

8/21/2016

Stressed and depressed,
but Halloweening but
upset and anxious
and c o n f u s e d
and Lost.

8/27/2016

I really need to start working on my writing. I keep putting it off. I have so many ideas, and have been experiencing so many fascinating dreams. I need to get it out. But I'm so lazy. I at least ought to keep up a dream journal. Goodness, I slept so much last night...about 18 hours...vivid dreams. I hope I can remember them when I actually have the patience to record them down. As of now, I'm a bit tipsy and don't feel like probing my mind for details. I have so much on my mind and so much to say, yet I sign off.

My signature looks weird.

8/28/2016
People are strange, Strange, and rude.

9/5/2016
Flies in our tea and knots in our stomach
Hot glued fingers and gems in the pocket

Sip and glue, set, place, and sigh
Bedazzled skulls don't want to die

Incense ash makes home of the carpet.
Hills on the desk, slide our fingers, define it

Watered down but we musn't waste
Dip your fingers; press that ash to paste

9/5/2016
SO FUCKING SCREWED.
NO MONEY.

11/18/2016
Currently sitting at Hot Shots, in Pismo. I accidentally ordered a pint instead of a liter of beer, but perhaps it was for the best? The liter always gets warm before I finish, so two cool pints probably are nicer. Ha! My creativity had gone stale. I get bursts of ideas; however, my drive to pursue in their expansions proves to be stubborn. It makes me anxious and depressed. My art is declining as well. I think part of it is the heat. I cannot focus well or thoroughly enjoy myself when it is the slightest bit warm (for it is not "hot" here, just warm, and my room absorbs all the heat of the day and holds it still, despite my fan and open window). I also need to take out all those filthy bottles. Then maybe the air will feel lighter. I know my stress is also holding me back. Money, housing, family turmoil, loneliness, etc...all are normal players in the game of misery. Ha! But I

guess the best word to describe how I am feeling at this moment is this: STALE.

11/30/2016

Shuffle on home, boy. Fast as you can, boy.
Play with your toy, boy. Feed your beast.
It's all alone, boy. While you have fun, boy.
Think how it feels, boy. Where it can't see?

Wet and moldy, cold and sad
To hear the laughter and fire crack
Eyes that stopped working,
Too long in the dark

Oh!
I'd give my life for one night in the park

12/8/2016

My god my stomach hurts.

1/9/2017

I'm an alcoholic. I know it. I hate it, yet I love it. I need to stop. I don't want to stop. I want to stop for my health, but I want to continue for the (obviously dangerous) momentary "high" it lends me. Withdrawal– I was in denial about it, but I know I've been feeling it: "trembling, shaky hands and legs, foggy mind and an inability to concentrate on anything." I feel like I'm failing at self control (I KNOW that). My poor liver, my heart, my stomach, what have I done?!! But I know that I still love it and depend on it and I can't promise myself that I won't die from it (like my Uncle Steve).

1/12/2017

FINALLY have a decent and somewhat elaborated novella/short story idea.

1/16/2017

I had been out of Pristiq for a couple days and had a major psychotic/manic episode this morning. I had to leave work to go to the pharmacy. $70 later, I had my meds. I was sick and still shaky for a good while, ready to vomit, but I held it down. It was scary and fascinating, feeling how I did in 2011, pre-hospitalization. It made me borderline angry

70

about how my creativity spikes during mania. I so wish my art and creative drive were as intense all the time. My medications tone it down, and it is quite frustrating. But the physical symptoms of being un-medicated convinced me that I need to stay on my meds. That self destructive tendency is so overwhelming. I was wanting to slice myself and drive off the edge of the highway. Or bash my head into the corners of countertops. I was on the verge of tears due to the heightened adrenaline. Paranoia. Nausea. I did not miss that feeling. I feel a little better, but part of it is from my drinking and promise of my self-harming if I feel like it (for I started self harming again in 2013). I have so much to convey, but I feel that it would be hours of writing to get everything down. For now, I drink and stress.

1/19/2017

Finalized that "Worm" song (sort of). Too bad my cello bow is broken and I spend all my money on alcohol instead of a new bow. I have what I want from the cello, which makes me even more frustrated. I know what I want, but I can't make it. Typical. I was able to organize my room a bit. I ate an orange and felt momentarily powerful.

I'm glad I found that voice memo thingy on my phone though. Will help me remember melodies and perhaps dreams (if I remember to use it).

1/20/2017

Dressing as different parts of myself doesn't mean I'm trying to be someone different. I am expressing a part of myself which I've felt on the inside for all my life. I am finally revealing it. It makes me feel like I am no longer hiding, regardless of the fact that I use make-up or wigs or "fake" names. This is me. These characters are inside my mind. They are me. And sometimes I like to let them out. I like to let myself be who I want to be. (Badly written— try to get the point across in a better way when you can, Emily Carol.)

Boozy Faces (?)

I know that they cause death. I know they're bad, but then they're not, on days I would have wept.

1/21/2017

Having my third drink of the day. I went to Harry's after work, and now I'm at Cool Cats. If I didn't do all this drinking, perhaps I'd actually be able to not leech off of my mom so I'll be able to pay my rent. I am so disappointed with myself. I hate it. I can't stand myself, and I feel as if any happiness of mine is not deserved. I hate my anxiety, but I feel that it is owed to me. I brought myself to this point. Of course my mental illnesses play a part, but, because of my understanding of them, I shouldn't allow them to overpower me as strongly as I let them. I acknowledge my irrational thoughts and habits. I acknowledge the steps I can start making to aid in bettering my coping choices. However, I allow myself the booze and the cigarettes and the razors and the napping. I allow myself to cease productivity for the sake of indulging myself to the point of self-disgust. I HATE MYSELF FOR IT, yet I know that, as I write this, hoping that I will be wise and start focusing on addressing my problems in a proactive, healthy manner, I will find myself being the same person tomorrow: tipsy and regretful. Dismissive and repellent to my own joys.

My not taking Celexa has helped my creativity, and I have found that there is an increase in motivation. Perhaps I was receiving too much serotonin? I am pleased, anyhow, in that regard. But, as I noted earlier, I feel that such pleasure is not deserved. I am still a horrible individual. Lazy and weak. Yes, as I also stated earlier, there are moments when my mental issues do overpower in a way that I really cannot control. But I still knowingly ruin myself when I have a coherent choice to make, which I choose to butcher with my shit decisions. Such self-loathing is trite. It is typical and nauseating. But there is a reason, is there not, that it has become so common in journals and literature, in films and television, in the minds of so many humans. I am not alone, as cliche as that statement is. And sometimes, that understanding makes me feel even more disgusted with myself.

However, C is visiting this weekend, and that makes me happy. =)

1/22/2017

I was going to go out to drink (again; I had a beer while waiting for my take-out ((because my money management is non-existent)), so I failed "not going out to drink as often"), but I ended up just walking around the block. I do suppose that I would have ended up at the bar had it not started pouring and soaking me. Ha! I loved the water, but I knew that I looked like a drowned rat. So I came back to my room to change. I drank some water and took my evening meds and a Xanax, and then I did some cleaning (whoa). Not much compared to what is done daily in an average household; however, small accomplishments such as that are rare for me. Pathetic. Again, as I mentioned in yesterday's entry, this slight confidence I feel at the moment, though I know it's exaggerated and temporary, is not deserved. I am still a lazy, unmotivated alcoholic with horrible self control. For I'm sure that I will end up going out for at least one more beer tonight.

I have some cold Pinot Grigio in the fridge, so I'll first see if that will satisfy my cravings. But there's always a fantastic satisfaction that is reserved for a crisp, cold beer straight from the tap. Goodness, writing about it is making the craving more intense. But I know that journaling is good for me. Maybe my dislike of people will keep me in, for there are some particularly obnoxious ones out tonight (although it could be that my patience is lower today. Ha!). Meanwhile, I shall listen to Oghr and try to get some creative projects worked on. Bleh.

1/22/2017
 It's G's Bday! <3

1/25/2017
 Once again, I am out drinking. Made it only two days without going to a bar. I am disgusted with myself. However, C is visiting tomorrow, and I am very much looking forward to that. I do feel I need to commit to working on projects; my laziness astounds even myself at times. And FUCK IT I need to get better at saving money. But I am drinking it tonight. TYPICAL (yeah). America is a mess, and it's making me sick. I feel like I'm in a dystopian novel. This country is a pile of gooey, oily shit.

1/25/2017
 I can't think of anything clever to say.

2/3/2017
 I'm 24 today! I am currently waiting in the laundromat. My head is weird since I drank after a few days of very light/no alcohol. What I do to myself! I'm trying to come up with a pitch for a horror movie for a contest, but I'm super anxious and disheartened currently, so all I've found is upset and frustration. I'm clammy and pudgy, and the world feels off. I need to unload my car and take out the trash, but I'm nervous for tourists to see me...I need to actually do things first thing, around 5am, but I'm LAZY. Back to the horror pitch: I think I have a decent idea, but everything feels so mundane and boring when I'm feeling the way I am feeling today. Perhaps I'll feel better later and will elaborate on the day.

2/12/2017
 I must elaborate on and continue the Marionette story. My lack of creativity is upsetting. Anxiety.
 I am sitting at the bar in Cool Cats, trying to be persistent in my constant attempt at creativity. However, my mind is dry. Perhaps it is the

post-mom-visit depression? Who knows. It makes me sad, borderline ill. I do have a surplus of ideas, but the energy and creativity needed to embellish such ideas is absent. Dull. Void. Stale.

It seems that this occurs when I finally think my imagination is ready to collaborate with me again. Maybe it's self sabotage. I do fully believe that I do not deserve any positivity that may come my way. Ill occurrences are mine, and anything else is...strange (poor word choice, I know, but my vocabulary and ability to accurately express myself is lacking) more often than not (and, please, pardon my trite expression), and, oh, how I've already forgotten what I was going to write at this moment: what a typical occurrence in this melancholy! Since I have forgotten my previous subject, I guess I ought to mention that I have, at the moment, decided that I want to finish my degree (Philosophy major and Creative Writing minor) at Warren Wilson. That school is always haunting me, and I miss it so much, and dream of it so much that I sometimes feel that I may cry when I remember it. I understand that my return to WWC is impractical, and that my undergraduate degree is long overdue, but I do think that graduating from Warren Wilson will bring me closure and help me prove to myself that I can finish at least some of the things I attempt.

2-22-17 (Dream)

Weird "sleep world"– lack of some motor movements, and strange sensory details. With my lucid dreaming tendency, I could manipulate some of the things that were happening– but it felt like there was always a strange "weight" pulling me from complete control. Weird house was there that I occasionally visit in my other dreams– I float rather than walk– and I know some parts of it are real and some are purely fragments from the dream "world" (you do not age while in that "dream dimension"). I met strange old woman–skinny with white hair– philosopher type. She showed me an improv-technique and we chatted about philosophy. Then she met me in the "real world" and brought me through a "door" to the dream dimension– it led to a HUGE room full of philosophy professors at a bar, playing pool, and discussing. I saw JC– my WWC advisor and professor. I joked with him– he was sitting at the bar. Then I followed the lady through a giant sliding glass door which led us out of the "philosophy room" and further into the "dream" dimension. At some point, the strange lady went mad– she began searching to find and kill a baby. The baby, my sister, brother, and I (and parents) were in a room full of rows of chairs. If your clothing does not match, you are blind while in the room. The woman was not matching, so she could not see the child that she was after. She tried to sense it, but it did not work. We all dashed out, passing the child through the door until we made it through the glass doors, across the philosophy room, and out of the entire "dream" dimension. I never saw the woman after that– though she was mentioned a few times.

2/22/17 to 2/23/17 (Dream)
There were two small "theatres"– I favored the second one. They played television shows, but projected them as if the scene were happening right in the room with the audience. Like, you could reach out and touch the actors and the set (feel their breath?). The decor, in both, were reminiscent of "ancient" designs. Again, I favored the design of the second. I had followed a brown haired girl into the second theatre, which was playing an episode of a television show. There were only a few of us, and we sat around the perimeter of the room. In a separate dream, my siblings and I were elected (somehow) into "high council" positions. The "city" was inside a GIANT dome. We were scrambling about– my brother disappeared entirely; I think he turned into a god, actually– not positive if that dog was him or not (he took the form of a canine deity I think). Then I guess the city became overrun by fascists who were after my siblings and I and who wanted to take control. Soon we and all the city dwellers were pursued by the people working for the guy trying to take control. I did not get out, and he lined us up and drilled us on history and made sure we knew that he had complete control. Me and the guy in the row parallel to mine managed to escape out of the "dome" and found ourselves in a city that looked dusty, run-down, and abandoned. Most homes were just skeletons. Apparently, if we stuck pencil lead into tiny holes in some of the buildings, a secret door would open and we could collect these weird looking metal things about an inch and a half long. I only collected three. I met up with some others who had escaped and were collecting the metal "keys" (that's what I thought of them as).

2/24/2017
Fresno wakes you up with a headache and ash under your fingernails.

2/24/2017
I had a "whirlwind trip" to Fresno and back. Left yesterday around 1pm and arrived back here in Pismo around 5pm today. My anxiety is nauseating, and I'm shaky. Of course I am now drinking at Cool Cats and waiting on food. My room in Fresno now brings me upset rather than comfort. I think it is because it is being used by others. Invaded. It no longer is my sanctuary. Perhaps upon my next return I'll start the process

of boxing up my stuff. Not out of pettiness, but because I think it's time. My food has arrived.

2/28/2017 (Dream)
(Out of order.)
My cats, except for Midnight, had died. I ventured into another dimension in which all the souls of the dead resided. It looked just like the "living world," but had an unsettling, dreamlike atmosphere about it, and when things moved, they left behind a slight blur– just a tad ghoulish/ghost-like. I could only bring back one soul, and I chose my late cat, Sunkist. There were suddenly crowds of people, bands performing, etc...(I was in a large garage). To the side was a shop, and a woman kept pulling out items (coats, shorts, shoes, etc...) saying I could pick two to bring back to the "real world" with me. Other people were offering me things to take back– perhaps it was some sort of test, or perhaps taking one of their items to the living world would empower them somehow?
Regardless, I refused all of their offers, explaining that I came for Sunkist and would only leave with Sunkist (I think if I took anything else, I could not have her back).

3/8/2017 (Dream)
These bits may be scattered and out of sequence– I am not recording my dreams right away, as I should, so bare with me. At some point, I was at a strange school (I think there was a tad bit of magic involved, for I think some other students and I were floating/flying). I was wandering with my coworker, E, and a couple others. At some point, there was a hurry to get up some very steep bleachers, and people were so eager that they trampled E and she fell through and I was the only one who could help her.

At another part, there was trouble going on in which people were "emptied" and were paraded by their captors like lifeless, braindead balloons; they were also followed by a type of security. I had made a strange bond with a guy who had performed a show I saw, and I found out he had been "emptied." He was being held captive by his mother, who, upon getting a heads up by security that I was coming, put her son in her trunk. I managed to make it to her and get to the body. However, the only way I could permanently wake him up was to attempt to have him make a waking connection within the first minute or less that I get his attention– otherwise, he would die completely. I managed to jog his memory/life by singing the song he performed in the show I saw him in.

In another segment, I had made (magically, I think) a weird, small, decorative sweater-like thing. A group of guys tore it apart and started to use the pieces for their own things. I think I had an attachment to the pieces I had used, so I was very upset and flew out of the room (literally). One of the guys had sort of been a friend of mine. I arrived later to my room with the sweater thing restored and a letter (brief) of an apology on his part. It also said that he loved me.

In yet another segment, my sister had a ginger boyfriend (English, too), and she got pregnant and gave birth. The building we were in kept morphing, though, and time was going by in different rooms and hallways, and her child kept being lost, and we would all set out to recover her child. There was rumor that her boyfriend caused trouble (purposefully) to many, but my sister would not believe it. She was right, and he somehow managed to get the building back to normal and recover their daughter.

In another segment, we were in a building. It was strange and we were all having trouble getting out and discovering the cause of the building's strangeness and the deaths/disappearances it caused. At some point, I think we had figured it out, although I don't remember what the resolution was. We were all trying to get out of the building for good, for it was destroying itself from the outside in. I got trapped and a fire broke out, but the floors were also flooding with water, and what the fire touched (water-wise) became deadly– not sure why. I was hopping along things and scaling walls and bannisters. At some point, there was a ship floating in the toxic water beneath me, and I tried to jump into it. However, it was a trick of the house and moved out of my way at the last second, causing me to almost fall into the water. I stood on a narrow ledge against a flat wall and eventually managed to jump onto a different little boat that randomly appeared.

3/24/2017 - 3/25/2017 (Dream)
Me and other people were traveling by way of a small, flying boat thing (we being the ones who powered it). It was simple and didn't have wings, so we all had some sort of power. Mine was momentary levitation (I could use it to catch a fall or lift me up to grab something, but it would not be strong enough to allow me to fly). My sister could create things by singing, but their survival time was not always known. Ex: she could create a wall to keep invaders out during a battle, but it would disappear anywhere between a couple minutes to centuries. (I think our short lasting creations were due to our being young and not having fully developed our powers.) There was a young boy, maybe 8 or 9 years old, who could come back to life (although we all had a feeling that there was a limit to his lives

and tried to keep him from jumping off high walls for fun, which he liked to do). There was a teenager (aged 17-19). I can't remember her power. There was another guy, around age 20-22, and I cannot remember his power right now. We all had similar power which we used to power our "boat." The more of us onboard that there were, the smoother the sailing. If we all fell asleep, the boat would crash (again, I think it is because our powers were not fully developed. Perhaps more people could keep it afloat as they slept). When I was trying to fly it alone, it kept tipping and wobbling and not wanting to go in the correct directions.

　　　　I WILL MAKE MORE NOTES ABOUT THIS DREAM AFTER I GET MY COFFEE.

　　　　It seemed that we had a temporary hub that looked like the top floor of an abandoned parking garage. The door normally leading to the staircase led to a stage theatre. They were currently performing Willy Wonka. On the other side, there was a similar door that led to a fast food restaurant. The young boy enjoyed jumping out of the parking garage and reviving himself. At some point I found dozens of racks of clothes (which is where I got the dark green dress from). I think, at some point, we got separated and I needed to "power" the "boat" on my own, which was difficult. It was hard to avoid telephone wires and traffic, as it did not want to fly high enough. At some point, I was "flying" my "boat" over a part of the ocean that was right next to a forest. The ocean water was calm, but I knew it was not a lake or a pond. There were stairs leading down into it in some areas, and at some point, it all widened into a HUGE, calm, clear pool, but I knew it was still the ocean.

3/28/2017
　　　　I'm feeling mildly suicidal. Is that even a thing? Mildly?
　　　　　　　　Cutting.
　　　　　　　　　　　　Cutting.
　　　　　　　　　　　　　　　　Fucking alcoholism.

　　　　Drinking drinking spending money cutting Tuesdays oh so funny

3/29/2017
　　　　Will I be able to pay my rent?

4/1/2017
　　　　OR WILL IT SINK WHERE IT SITS?

4/3/2017

Here I am, once more, drinking. I didn't drink at all yesterday, and last week I went two days in a row with no alcohol, all for money reasons (why else? Ha!). Mom's birthday is on Friday, and I am unsure as to whether or not I should make a trip to Fresno. I feel guilty even questioning it...the drive is getting so monotonous. Oh, and I am terribly behind on my recording of my dreams. Ahhhh. Typical.

4/15/2017

I am super dissociated today. Strange, vivid dreams...so much sleep, and I cannot entirely wake my mind up. The sunlight is weird, and 70% of me is not awake. Things are floating and I am not all real, but the senses I recall most and still feel currently are those from the memories of my dreams. I am recalling one right now, am in it. Feeling it. The stale food and the fresh water and the clothes and the painting. I am there more than I am here, and part of me wants it to remain so. But how long can this be okay? My body is cleansing itself and my stomach churns and my bowels sigh, and I am empty, but for feeling the dreams and the dissociation— so strange that "dissociation" can be used to describe a feeling. Ha! Paradox. I must record recent dreams and worlds, but there are so many and I have not enough time to do them justice in writing. Hand can't move so quickly. Need, perhaps, a recorder. My bowels call again and so do my dreams. I shall return?

Dream bullets (no order or connection used in arrangement):
- Weird ("virtual reality") train/spaceship game/ride with different levels, but was actually very real.
- Large mansion hosting a convention/huge gathering: celebratory? Upon arrival, we were given some wardrobe choices and accessories to choose from (the gathering, I believe, was primarily centered around Doctor Who). I could not get my necklace to look right.
- Somehow connected to the "spaceship/train ride." I was being followed and forcefully guided on my journey through the levels. It seemed to span several years. But, apparently, once I completed everything, I could return to the "real" world with no time having passed, but my memories of my adventures and aging would still exist, but I will be a child again. I lamented to my "captor" about not wanting to have to grow up all over again, especially since I would have mentally already done so. I also remember being strangely drawn to my captor.

- That one street that I've visited multiple times in my dreams, and can often will myself to find, has a cool, cluttered bookstore, delicious tea shop/parlor, hidden side streets and shops only accessed by going through abandoned sections and narrow alleyways. The shop (goth-psychedelic) with clothing on the ground floor, and strange, glowing (under blacklight?) decorative items in the basement area of the shop. Bongs used as flower vases sitting on a glass table by leather couches.

Why can't I remember anything when I am in the mindset/have the patience to record things? Perhaps, when dissociated, because my mind is not completely "grounded" in reality and the (my) present waking existence, my recollection of my dreams and "fugues" is stronger and tangible. When I am more clear minded, and out of my "dream world," my connection with my non-waking "reality" (for it is very real to me more often that I think is healthy) is not strong at all. I really need a voice recorder, but I am incapable of prioritizing my finances even though I've been wanting a voice recorder for quite a while and could really benefit from it.

4/16/2017

I must begin to focus on my writing and my art. However, I say this constantly and never accomplish anything from it. I am lazy, and I am also tired, although I have no reason to be. So many thoughts in my mind, and so little attempts to get them out, to record them. And is it then my disappointment which further prevents me from pursuing my creative attempts, perhaps? The uncertainty only aids to my confusion and self-loathing, which I believe to be valid. I have even programmed a reminder to work on one of my stories. It goes off every day at noon. However, I have not once worked on the project since putting the reminder into my phone. Self sabotage? Laziness? Lack of talent? Lamenting my lack of talent? Perhaps a blend. I do understand that, regardless of whether or not I actually have talent at my passion (writing), I should still pursue it. It has always been me. Cheesy. True. Stop being such a loser, and stop not only disappointing others, but stop disappointing yourself as well. Until then, finish your beer, Emily.

5/1/2017

A year ago from tomorrow will be the one year mark of my working at the bakery. I just spent nearly a week up in Fresno, during which I was able to see my family perform Bach's Mass in B Minor (The Fresno Grand Master Chorale). It was amazing! I brought my dear friend,

MJ, along as well– such a jolly good time. Now I am back in Pismo. I am feeling something a bit like vertigo– I think it must be a blend of strange med mix-ups (ran out– been taking half-doses, etc...on trip ((I forgot to bring refills on my trip))). My head feels funny and I am a bit dissociated. I am also quite nauseous. And sweaty. Very gross. But I ordered a beer and some "frings" (fries and onion rings) after taking the proper dosage of my evening meds, so I'm hopeful that my mind will clear a bit.

5/3/2017
"Worm" by Emily Carol (Updated)

Inside out or outside in
Let him, please, sometime crawl in
He needs food– you're quite the bite
So won't you let him feast tonight?

Kind and soft
Teeth so long
Will always thank you with a song

He wiggles down your throat, so tight
To find some meat that smells just right
He's fond of muscle, slurps up lard
His favorite: tender, pulsing hearts

Kind and soft
Teeth so long
Will always thank you with a song

Inside out or outside in
Let me please, sometime, crawl in
I need food– you're quite the bite
So won't you let me feast tonight?

I'm kind and soft
My teeth are long
And nibble, nibble, slowly, 'til you're gone!

5/13/2017
"L" siblings' (my BFFs) Graduation! MJ joining too! San Jose.

5/30/2017 (Dream)

I was in my 4-8 year old body, but was aware of my current age and memories.

6/2/2017

"Kid's show" which involves characters that come out of a shower curtain "image"– girl gets pulled into it, in the end the family moves out and an older man moves in. Shower curtain stored away? Burned?

6/8/2017

I am financially doing better and hope to continue that way. I do need to get back into recording in my spending log; however, I am worried for my friend, MJ, as she is going through some dark times, but I will try my best to be there for and to keep an eye on them. My dear "Marwood." Ha! I need to start working on my writing and art– I know I continually mention this. Oh well. I guess I should first focus on my ever-growing errands I need to run tomorrow.

6/13/2017

Screenplays to get:
* *Benny and Joon*
* *Ghost World*
* *Harold and Maude*
* *American Mary*
* *Naked*

6/14/2017

SPIDERS (I keep finding them on and around me.) <3

The only job I've had where I didn't end up crying in the bathroom was my library job.

Super depressed today. Bad stomach and intestine pain. BUSY weekend ahead (car show), and I'm already disappointing my boss and coworkers. I do this to myself, and I never stop, even when situations like this continue to happen.

7/11/2017 (Dreams)

Dreams from Sunday night, 7/9/17 → Monday morning, 7/10/17: I cannot remember the majority of the details, as I, stupidly, did not record them as soon as I awoke– the details will be recorded here out of order, and, most certainly, with many parts missing (unfortunately):

The dream took place at some sort of boarding school– grounds were very large and seemed very expensive and prestigious. There was obviously something very dark and horrible occurring and there were many accidents (and some fatalities) that kept happening. My friends and I (I know one was MJ and one other was my sister, L (who at some point ended up pregnant in that "world"...like I saw her future and there were pregnancies and babies in it) were in our group– but we were all round 12-14 years old...closer to 12, now that I think about it. At one point, we were trapped in this huge, tall, enclosed, metal staircase– the stairs attached at all different places–sometimes we had to climb through bars/jump/crouch/etc...to get to the next set of stairs. We were trying to find our way out: we had been "locked in" as we were investigating something we found curious. At one point, a girl (about 19-22?), pregnant, was frantically trying to find her way out (not sure how long she had been there– we kind of stumbled upon her). She saw a window, but it was covered in bars and she could not fit through to escape (narrow bars and too high up). The scene shifted, and I could tell we were close to the exit. The pregnant girl was very upset and jumped from a pipe that ran along the wall– falling down down down to where the stairs began– hundreds of feet! I heard the heavy thud and crack of her bones. We exited and saw an older woman (her mother) who was frantically asking about her and freaking out. We told her that she had killed herself, and the mother broke down. I felt awkward but was, otherwise, unaffected.

However! This next character I am to introduce is one that has haunted me since I dreamed of her! She was about 12? Long brown/red/auburn hair, partially pulled back. She wore cute, strange clothes and enjoyed strange trinkets and types of things from stores such as "as seen on TV." The weird mall in that dream world had a sort of "hidden" shop, and that is where she found most of her strange toys/things ~ one was a weird camera which was a huge pair of plastic, green goggles, and when you blinked a certain way, it would take a picture and print a polaroid. She also had a collection of strange collectibles– pins, earrings, pendants, posters, comics, prints, necklaces, etc... She enjoyed gifting and trading them. She had them set up, extravagantly, in her closet (a huge walk in. The front of the closet door had a large, square mirror hanging on the front). Anywhoo, she was strange and lovely, but apparently was involved in some way with the bad things that were going on. They were messing with her, and she started getting upset a lot.

I'm not sure what caused the final "act," but it was due to something that happened to another group/person/her family/etc...I DON'T KNOW– wish I DID. I wasn't there, but, as it was my dream, I saw it happen: she killed herself– shot? Combusted at will? I'm not too sure. She was standing in front of her closet mirror. When she died, it did not shatter, but matted over. A weird silhouette of her was left, surrounded by blood spatter (but all the reflective abilities of the mirror were gone). I found her, I think. Her death upset me so much, and still does! She was such a good, pure, loving person, and she was gone, and it hurt so much– for me both in my dream and even now. She lay there, and I situated what was left of her body to look as peaceful as possible. My friends found us and we were all distraught and confused and outraged, as we knew this was linked to the other bad things that were happening. I remember reflecting on the odd stoicism she showed leading up to her death– perhaps that had been why I went to check on her (therefore discovering her body). We knew that her death would be covered up– so we immediately decided to not stop trying to figure out what was going on. The people in charge found us with her body (but how did they know to come to her room?!). They took her away, and, by the next day, had cleared out most of her things. Her mirror and the contents of her closet now remained, and we all dispersed them amongst us– as she would have wanted. I took her mirror– now it was a strange "portrait."

The next day, as we were taking the last of her belongings, we heard a tour going on in her room (we were all hidden in the closet). The people in charge were explaining (to clients?) about the new space and its possibilities. I exited and confronted them, angry. Why were they ignoring what happened? Why weren't they surprised? What role did they have? In her death? In all the other deaths? Etc... I do not remember the outcome of that outburst, however. I time-jumped to the end of my stay at whatever that place was. I was organizing and packing up my room. I picked up a trinket I had chosen from her closet (I think it was some sort of pendant...?). I turned and looked at her mirror. It was propped up against the foot of my naked bed. The overwhelming sadness and hurt felt in my dream and even now is astounding (and, the next morning, I learned that my coworker's sister-in-law passed away unexpectedly). Even now, two days later, the death of the girl in my dream makes me hurt so, so much.

7/14/2017
"I enjoy how much you don't care."

8/11/2017

The past several weeks have been tedious. Besides my friends' visiting, it has all been a jumble of total hosh-posh and nonsense. My car was repossessed, and then, a week later, it died– it is fixed and working lovely now, however. Perhaps the repo was what triggered this bout of depression. And from then on, anything that may have once been minor now presents itself as something major, causing my mind to wilt and my already pathetic motivation to dwindle. I feel like a sick, sweaty pigeon (can birds sweat) with missing feathers and no home, flapping around with no destination. I've been cutting more often than I have in the past several months— and in larger "portions." I feel fat and tired, and my anxiety holds my heart and squeezes tight when I feel I may be about to have a moment of normality (which, for me, is just mild depression, but with no heart palpitations or maddening anxiety attacks, psychosis, or dissociation). I was interviewed for the news, which I regret so— if they only used my voice, I may feel better, but seeing myself as others do, with my big, squinty, blotchy face, stupid, flat hair, huge chin, and fat, gross, slumped body has made these past few days miserable. I can feel myself regressing and the Emily from Summer 2008 appears and I want to stop eating and stop being gross and start making myself something that isn't chubby and gross and ugly. I know that a lot of what I feel and desire is linked to my mental illness, but I find that I do not care. I'm always paranoid and anxious and depressed. (I still take my meds, but meds do not erase an illness— though many stupidly think that of them.)

What I'd need to treat what I am currently dealing with is therapy— a thought that, of course, gives me anxiety. Numbers— times— appointments— commitments~ my heart screams at the mention of them. Yet numbers and time and appointments and commitments are now the foundation of most everything. This is maddening. I love numbers, and I also love my fascination and their relationship with me. It is perplexing. An addiction (separate from my alcohol— ha!). But I am surrounded by and have to deal with them constantly— and so the obsession is always... "activated" within me, mentally and physically. And now I am rambling and am causing anxiety to stir and stir as it counts and my heart thumps, and I so wish I could better articulate what I feel and what I want and everything else— for there are so many layers (and each with their own layers) to this number/time/etc...obsession. I must stop for now. And I must invest in a voice recorder. That would make things a bit easier when my hand cannot write as fast as my mind thinks. I may explode.

~Help~

8/12/2017

When I say "tiny existence," I do not mean social status, race, income, profession, etc... I say "tiny" in regards to thought: to not understand, or, at least, to not have even the desire to understand. When I say "tiny," I mean that potential thought and understanding is ignored. Unobserved. Something pushed aside, often because the problem may not inconvenience one personally, or because it simply does not matter to one. A person can travel and school themself but not exist wholly if they do not recognize more than the "tiny" things. Empty. Plain. Simple. Pitiful. Detestable.

Humanity is lacking.

8/30/2017

Depressive day! Work went well (strange, for a Wednesday), but the melancholy always finds me. I've been using Xanax and alcohol to help me sleep, but my anxiety is still often high. It's hot (hot for the coast), which doesn't help. I'm hungry but I'm scared of food. I need to take out my seven months of trash, but I'm lazy and gross. I need to work on my writing and art, but I'm pathetic and horrible at following through with anything that may prove beneficial to my well-being. I'm even too lazy to write journal entries as often as I originally planned to (and should). My dreams, however, have become more vivid and "theatrical" than they have been in a while, which is good (and likely caused by the mixture of excessive Xanax, booze, sleep, and, maybe, a subconscious yearning to develop some sort of story). Ha! Oh well.

10/9/2017 (Dreams)

L and I were very close twins.

There were elevators with coded ways to get to floors. Weird stairs. Upper level is posh and has special currency. We went undercover and were, at first, caught in a bathroom, but we changed clothes. Multiple kids dispersed throughout the building— and most were killed, as was the man trying to help hide us. We had to be separated at one point as part of our undercover (we had to marry some random guys). We had previously sought shelter with other children, but a raid happened and we all scattered and hid in bathtubs.

10/10/2017 (Dream)

A tall, dark-haired Asian gal and a tall, long-haired light brown haired Caucasian gal are friends. The brunette is an aspiring writer. The Asian gal's best friend had been killed and she agrees to let the brunette be her new best friend as long as the brunette promises not to ask her to read/preview her writing as she was not fond of reading. I interacted with them as a disembodied spirit who helped humans to communicate with a Goddess (not sure why or how). I floated around and followed my sister (who was still alive and the only one who could see me). I pranked people, too. It was fun being like a ghost.

12/20/2017

This will be brief, but, as I have not written here in over two months, I feel that anything is "worthwhile." I hate myself, as usual. I have more ideas for some writing– ways to flesh out some of my pre-existing ideas, and I hope to address such ideas soon. Maybe I'll actually start accomplishing some writing. Boy howdy! I'll try to elaborate on my poor existence soon. But, as I am tired, both from life and beer, and hungry, both from life and beer, I shall retire for now.

12/27/2017

I write the same thing over and over and over. Redundancy is my calling, I assume. Again, for example, I find myself plagued with a self-disgust caused by my lack of creative initiative. I know that if I actually studied and sat myself down to work on my writing, I would make some sort of progress, even if only for my "peace of mind." I don't wish to write to be famous. Yes, I would love to leave some impact on readers, but I firstly want to release my thoughts– get them out and feel like I've completed something– which I don't believe I ever have. Perhaps, even with the "completion" of some stories, I will find that no story will actually "end" end, which is cliche, but very likely– I'm scattered now. And my use of words is poor. My ability to sound mildly decent is dying and, honestly, probably never existed in the first place. I'm only aware of it now. UGH. Pity party whine whine sulk and grimace: I am good at those things. I excel. Ha!

I am currently waiting for E, B, M, and their mother to arrive in Pismo– they are stopping on their way back to Fresno. I hope they arrive soon. I miss them.

My anxiety is high.

I feel as if I linger too often and will soon become an awkward nuisance– maybe I already have. That weird one who won't go away, but is pitied and so is tolerated so as not to have their feelings hurt. But I am also aware that I despise myself and always assume the worst.

To be continued.

12/29/2017

My depression and anxiety is disgusting today. I felt and still feel like crying– I can feel that weight and sinus pressure that comes with the

87

weeps of depression. And I actually, now that I am alone, would like to cry. Perhaps it would help release some of the grossness and self-disgust I feel. However, I can't cry. Like, I physically cannot cry. I'm just stale and nothing is able to be released. I want to cut so badly, but I think I only have one band-aid, and, also, now that L is staying with me, I don't want to risk her seeing anything (although my stomach will be my go-to if I definitely can't hold back). I'm getting a cold, I think. And I've been around some upset people recently, which always makes me feel a bit compromised. It's like I absorb some of their negative emotions, which makes my symptoms even stronger/worse. Like an emotional hangover. I really want to take tomorrow off, but I've been a horrible employee, and have been working half the amount of my normal hours. I'm letting people down– I've been given responsibilities and good words, but I don't deserve any of it. I'm just not sure if I can make it through tomorrow. When I'm like this, people looking at me and eye contact in general makes me want to cry. I can't get enough air and my heart palpitates, and, at that point, Xanax only helps a tiny bit. I'm exhausted, but I can't nap. Even with more Xanax and alcohol, I just hover, freaking out, and my throat is putty and I can feel all my skin and bones and organs and can smell every part of myself. During my panic attack on Sunday (12/24), I had auditory hallucinations– mainly music. It was so real and made me remember how things were in 2011. I don't know if the green comforter and memories of A have heightened it (and, today, one of my coworkers was wearing a similar body spray to A's, which may not have helped my situation), but it may have been adding to at least some of the anxiety. And the money and unproductivity, of course, is a constant shame for me– nothing new there.

      I'm also crushing on someone.

      I may ask for tomorrow off and give my never-ending apologies. I just feel so horrible doing that! Every time! It's so often! I'm eventually going to (if not already) be seen as a flake. A faker. An undependable, lazy complainer who can't handle anything remotely uncomfortable. I hate myself so much! SO MUCH. And even with the Xanax, wine, and spiced rum I'm working on at this moment, I doubt I'll be able to sleep. NO PEACE. But I don't deserve rest. Not until I actually do something right and work all my scheduled hours and take my trash out and get my tires checked and get my financial rut taken care of (as it is all my fault). UPDATE: I may take tomorrow off– I have a very understanding manager. I still feel guilty about it, however.

      Cutting is superb. So much that I can't spell. Ha! Cigarettes and beer and scary stories on Youtube. And then soon a good book (*Moon Palace* by Paul Auster).

KILL ME. mmm cringe
Sooooo 2011

1/20/2018
  I had been feeling much better, both physically and emotionally, since last Saturday. And I suppose I still am— I'm just dealing with getting some *feelings* under control soon.
  (constant ((UGH)) discontent)
  I have a lot to do which is making me feel like putrid sludge juice-trash needs to be taken out, tires aired and rotated, xmas gifts, bday gifts,applications and registration, bakery scheduling and communication, etc... And it is my own laziness that is keeping such things from being accomplished for MONTHS. So yes, with my improved emotions and physicality as mentioned above, I'm not as disgusted with myself as I have been, but I am still extremely upset, disappointed, and repulsed nevertheless. (And I won't even begin to dwell upon my lack of creative accomplishment— that would be too long an entry. Or perhaps I am just so terribly lazy and impatient to elaborate. Ha!).

1/23/18 (Dreams)
  Captor pretends to be another prisoner and "goes through" the situation alongside the real prisoner/victim.

  $3 movie theatre with pool and showers.

  Secretary that helps the dead develop their will post-death (if they never got around to it in life)— it will then manifest to the living.

  "The pain we've known.It echoes.Everlasting.Our ways been shown.Forever.Clouds are.gone.no.Or dawn.The breeze.Until.The sky's divided.Good night.Good night.Close.the mind.Escape to shore.Goodnight.Goodbye.Gone to fly.Until morn."

  A girl is brought back by her friend. Unfortunately, it is only temporary, and, in the end, she must go back to her death.

  Two close people can never meet face to face because both are locked up. They communicate with letters which they fly to each other in the form of a paper bird.

Two girls meet and begin dating while also having online relationships with anonymous users which turn out to be each other.

A character in a painting seems to be alive. Someone who doesn't care for it tries to destroy it and the character comes out to get "revenge."

A boy has an angelic voice. He is attacked and loses his ability to speak. He soon kills himself, but sings after death.

A gal named Helen brings her stories to life. Pretty soon, many dangerous things are released and people try to force her to kill off all of her characters. She does not want to; she does not believe it's right to take something's life away. So many people try to kill off Helen, thinking that it would get rid of the creatures.

A girl/boy always speaks of his/her family to her/his friends, only to return to an empty home every night. There really is no family.

A strange, mystical girl climbs out of a well, only to find herself in a strange world unlike her own. She is fascinated with the world she discovers, but remembers her family telling her that humans are dangerous and cruel. When she feels she can trust the world, she spreads her wings and flies, only to be shot down.

A girl talks to herself (future) over the internet/text.

A girl meets an unknown sibling over the internet.

"Be present with Earth."

4/19/2018
Work is so stressful and everyone is mad at each other and I am not doing anything right and I'm absorbing all the emotions around me and it's making me emotionally and physically ill.
Feeling very ill all the time now, due to work and life and all those other wonderful things. If I could, I would hurl myself into a black hole. But right now, that is impossible for me to do.

4/25/2018 (Dream)
A place that many forget about until they re-enter it. They must somehow leave notes for themselves so that they know to return. (After a

certain point, they may remember?) They'll sometimes dream about it or have flashbacks.

Maybe a library or bookstore– all currency welcome. Simply will not remember where the book came from, but books are read and continue to exist outside of the bookstore/library– if the library, they remember to return when the due date draws nearer. They are "coerced" into checking out materials when they wander into the library. Occasionally has parties– invitations sent to all who have visited.

Any notes written in an attempt to remember the library turn black after leaving.

5/16/2018

I've been looking more like myself lately– a good thing! Effort into clothes and make-up. Still depressed and getting fat, though. Ha! Running errands with L today. Denny's first! Then I may go to a cemetery or bother S or something. :)

Bad dream about a school shooting: Dead, injured, and frightened bodies. Shocked. Survivors reaching for help. "Rescuers" retrieve a gun from the shooter's body and hold it and kiss it and comfort it.

5/23/2018

Bands:
Bitter Ruin
The Great Malarkey
The Roaring Girl Cabaret
Caravan of Thieves
Katzenjammer

6/21/2018

I'm currently waiting for the UPS person to arrive. Apparently, I have to sign, and it requires waiting on the stairs and spending hours staring at the door to my building. Boring. And I'm very hungry and anxious.

I felt as if I was surrounded by death yesterday. The previous night, I dreamt that a family member was homicidal. I also dreamt that S's father had passed away– however, I have never met him. But it may have been a mother? (In the dream, S was getting prepared for someone's memorial). Then, the next morning, I drove by an accident on the highway that involved at least 7 vehicles. There were many emergency vehicles, and traffic was horribly backed up. But it was the traffic going in the opposite direction as me– North instead of South. I am not aware of if there were any deaths, but, either way, it was still a bit concerning. Then, as I was walking across the parking lot from Chase to Walmart, I found myself near so many crows (I LOVE crows, and I don't believe them to be evil or negative, but that, on top of all my other experiences from that morning, disturbed me a little).

Of course I found myself melancholy for the rest of the day. I mean, I understand that I am always melancholy, but it had a different "heaviness" to it yesterday. After all my excursions, I–

(pardon the interruption– my package came! It's an awesome Alice in Wonderland mug from G)

– lingered at home, despite my desire to linger elsewhere. I am now doing laundry, and the Sun hits my back like an angry fan. That doesn't make sense. I went to pet the cat at the bookstore and ended up purchasing three philosophy texts– all worn copies, which I love. They weren't too expensive, so I don't feel insanely guilty about spending money on them– only simply guilty.

A girl was just excited that I was writing in a diary. She said, "I have a secret diary." It was adorable. As I've written many times, I'm going to try to work on my writing more. L is much more active in her search for a new place to live, which means I'm also closer to having my "art corner" back– not that having limited space is a good excuse to not work on any of my projects– it is simply an easy one. I am, after all, lazy.

I always feel like that kid whom everyone rolls their eyes at when they see him enter the room, and whom people are nice to only out of either obligation or pity. I feel bad, and I do hate myself for being a pest to the people whom I care about. I often think about how some awkward people are not aware of how awkward and annoying they are, and so they can genuinely enjoy the interactions that they force upon others. What a calm existence– enviable. However, I do think I'd prefer my melancholic awareness even though it adds exponentially to my self hatred– at least I can tell when I really need to back off. I mean, I always feel unloved and like some sort of singing mosquito that gives everyone rashes, but I am aware of when the rashes are getting infected and I need to back off for a while.

I want to swim. Maybe I'll swim in the ocean after laundry and the shoe store or something. Even though I feel fat and gross. And anxious. *Always anxious.*

Will hopefully write here more often.
I feel horrible and I'm gross and lazy.

6/27/2018

I've been having some interesting dreams— not that that's unusual; however, I've lately become more inspired to work them into some of my creative projects. I have a dream from last night whose notes I'll most likely attach in here (perhaps I'll glue an envelope here and then place them in it). I don't want to lose my original scrawlings from first thing in the morning. I enjoy looking at that horrid handwriting.

I've been feeling better today. The wild dream helped quite a bit, I believe. I woke up around 7:30ish and it's 3:10 and I haven't given into a nap. This is a huge accomplishment for me, since all I've done this past week is sleep. I also feel like my dressing more like myself is helping my mood, even on my really bad days. This realization is the only thing keeping me from completely loathing myself for purchasing so many new clothes and accessories.

The beach is windy and people are hovering by my bench— out of all the benches to hover by! Mine must be sublime. The red buoy is out, which I hate, but I just had a bee come up to me, so that's good. It's cute.

Oh! I have some spider friends in my studio (whom I spend way too much time watching, talking to, and talking about). Greta is in the kitchen. Delilah is in my right-side room's left window, and Siouxsie, Banshee, Mercy, and Cindy Lou are in the window to the left of Delilah's. I love them. I always had dreams that I got a spider tattoo on the top of my left wrist. So now I really want one. Ha!

As always, I want to try to spend more time on my creative projects rather than sulking and lamenting the fact that I'm annoying and neurotic and shouldn't attempt further relationships. I just can't decide on the project I want to focus on right now. I think I want to connect some of my ideas— and I'll need to look at all of my notes and dream recollections to make those decisions. Some will also require research and more philosophy reading (which is fine and enjoyable— just very time consuming). I feel too dumb and uneducated to pursue certain stories, but I know it's better for me to at least attempt them.

(What's up with all these people hovering around my bench?) ← So many other benches available.

I bought a cow plushie today and I named her Anna (both after Annabelle and after anorexia). Fun fact

Maybe I'll just rewrite my dream notes after all. My handwriting is quite hard to read. I'll still hold onto the originals, of course.

Parts of the dream are missing, different, and out of order due to a trouble with recollection. I'll add in other details as I remember them. If I can. Ha!

(It's too windy and people are hovering, so I'm going to relocate before I rewrite the notes on my dream.) I still plan on recording my dream here. But first I must lament:

I feel so depressed. I feel so annoying. My feelings are often juvenile. I just hate that I am feeling. Sometimes I think I'd rather be numb. Of course, this does, in a way, give me a reason to put all of my focus and energy into my creative projects. I'm so distracted. I feel badly that people put up with me. I am not a good person. I'm trying hard not to hang around people too much anymore. Pretty sure it's better. I know I'm weird, annoying, neurotic, crazy, obsessive– and I know that people should dislike me. I just, of course, wish to be genuinely liked sometimes. It hurts.

Dream from Tuesday (6-26-18) → Wednesday (6-27-18): The Mall

Someone named Andy works in a shop and likes a girl who worked in the opposite side of the mall. MJ was there, but she occasionally changed appearances. Sometimes, the mall would "glitch" and someone could find themself "behind the scenes" and see weird "people" (they looked like humans, but they were out of focus and glitchy, a little robotic looking...) who sweep the area and capture people if they get stuck there. The shops are sometimes full of "demons" (demon meaning, here, a non-human spirit...not good or evil...just existing in their realm) who reside permanently "behind the scenes" in the alternate versions of each store. I think some of them used to be humans who got stuck there. I think that you don't get stuck, permanently, "behind the scenes" during a "glitch" unless one of the "people" finds you. Maybe they are alerted when a "glitch" happens. They (the "people") don't walk, but kind of slide and are more mannequin/cyborg-like. They'll sometimes throw the "captured" into the entryways of the "demon" stores; once near, the entities pull the human in and trap them, bodies turning into a blend of thick vapor and human entrails.

I was in a glitch, but another one happened within a couple seconds, just as a "person" began to slide towards me.

When "behind the scenes" you have to stay on the main pathway or you may explode into ash. However, the "people" frequent the main pathways.

L was there before me to try to create a written record of what was going on compared to what people were saying was going on, but her journals would often disappear or go blank. She eventually started acting oddly...twitching and zoning out...and eventually disappeared entirely.

("Behind the Scenes" existed everywhere, apparently...not just the mall.)

A woman in her 30s(?) with long brown hair and blue eyes was caught in a "glitch" and was taken by a "person." She was not thrown into a "demon" store, but was instead taken to an office. It was dimly lit by a secretary's computer screen. The secretary sat at a cluttered desk. L's missing journals and other similar reports were piled up from so many trying to record about "glitches" and "behind the scenes" and the "people." The secretary calmly looked at the woman but did not quit her work; she was typing vigorously. Cameras lined some areas and fed to a monitor to show both "sides" of the mall (real world and alternate world side by side). Was there a button to press should a "glitch" bring any visitors? The woman locked herself in a small room to the side of the office. A phone rang for a while, and when she finally answered it (it was the secretary, but the woman did not know that) there was just a weird mumbling/buzzing that somehow translated into thoughts in her mind. The secretary was giving her advice on how to escape. The woman pushed a desk aside. There was a makeshift window/door (looked a bit like a doggy door) in the wall near the floor. She crawled through it.

(Are all "workers" behind the scenes inhuman, or were some once human?)

I think a big group was trying to get through the mall to investigate or escape from something (for some reason, there were a lot of toddlers). At some point, MJ, Andy, and I joined them to help. My mom was there, too; I think it was right after L disappeared. My mom could only find one of her journals. It was a small, red one, but the words would blur or disappear whenever anyone would try to read them or were just entirely blacked out. (Andy disappears/dies after trying to decipher the journals too long.)

There was another "glitch" and a giant, dark fog rolled towards us, capturing and killing all who got caught in it. There was a weird barrier, and we were almost done lifting everyone over, but some adults and many toddlers were left stuck on the other side and disappeared in the fog, which stopped rolling at the barrier. Some of the group who had previously journeyed beyond the mall "behind the scenes" were in a mountainous/rocky area, and there were weird creatures. They were looking for two brothers. One ended up being crushed and eaten by something and the other was found alive but senile.

The woman who escaped through the wall door discovers a "hub." I think she had been separated from her husband during a "glitch" at the mall. I knew she had been unhappy with him about something and regrets the way they parted.

At one point a massive creature attacks and destroys all of our bodies, but we still, somehow, and over a long, long time, kill it and it turns to stone and crumbles.

7/3/2018 (Dream)
Music box filled with synchronized lights.

8/10/2018
I hate myself, so I punish myself for everything: happiness, sadness, eating, cutting, loving, etc... I'm tired and lonely and am tolerated out of obligation. I'm a poor friend, and am annoying. Easily replaceable. All I do is complain and lament, and people are probably growing more and more tired of it and me. I am cutting more often— it never feels like enough. But I want to swim and so I cannot cover too much of my body. I am suicidal, and daydream about death. The only thing keeping me alive is the fact that I don't want to put my mom through losing a child. She has already lost so many loved ones; it would break her.

So nothing fatal. Yet.

Also, death costs a lot.

It's a burden on others and myself to live, but also a burden on others to die.

8/29/2018
I find myself very confused, which is silly because what I am confused about are not very unusual ailments. There are just strange (or not so strange?) pieces that blend together strangely which makes the situation strange. I feel like a giddy, dramatic, obsessive pre-teen without reason. And I am quite petty. It's ridiculous because I don't want to even record my issues because I know that I will be embarrassed for myself if I or someone else were to read them in the future. Somehow using messy handwriting makes me feel a little better about sharing things in a journal. I, of course, need to start focusing on my writing and my art— haven't I been stating this in every entry? I will elaborate on my childish woes when I am not in public.

9/7/2018
Of course, I never did elaborate on what I was beginning to write about in my previous entry. Not sure that I will. My head is floaty and my eyes aren't working right. I understand that it is because I have not been really eating. I haven't had alcohol in nearly three days, and the cravings are intense— perhaps I will give in? I have about $5 until Wednesday. But

maybe a can of beer would be a worthy investment. Ha. I've also continued to self harm. It helps a lot, but it's getting annoying– having to wear longer sleeves all the time. Sweaty. And obvious. All my entries are the same. A mundane existence. Worthless. But dying is expensive, and I don't want to put that financial burden on anyone. I'm a pain alive and I'm a pain dead.

Ha!

10/5/2018

I was happy for a moment, so that makes it bearable.

6/7/2019

I very rarely understand myself, and I spend the majority of my time in a fog or depressed or confused. I don't trust any (well, most) of my feelings and perceptions, as I understand (one of the few things I understand...) that I am over-sensitive, paranoid, and easily discouraged.

May I find focus and peace and balance and understanding one day.

Most likely not.

On a separate subject, I am wanting to focus on my writing. However, the amount of times that I have made journal entries commenting on my hope to produce actual content is limitless and, honestly, a bit discouraging, as I still have not gone far with anything creative. It's disgusting to me, and adds to my distaste for myself. I want to write, paint, go to conferences, volunteer at libraries, etc... but I nap and obsess over love instead.

I am confused and disappointed.

I hope that I begin to actually improve myself and develop integrity in regards to my creative dreams– (S has really inspired my heightened intent to begin focusing on such projects, and I admire and respect him so much for that).

I am all over the place, but writing it down has made me feel slightly calmer. I know that my worries and situations are dreadfully common. I am not so different from most. I need not really complain. I need not feel special. I need really to just focus on what I want writing and art-wise. I am not as busy, and fill much of my excess time allowing my mind to create unnerving scenarios and deceptions to cripple me.

I must learn to calm down.

It is difficult.

9/7/2019

It has been a good amount of time since I went through my darkest experience (so far...ha); I am ready to go through my 2011 journal and reflect upon my entries. I think it will help me find some resolution, and, perhaps, allow me to further understand what may have been happening— for mental illness, when untreated, can surely whisk one far, far away from reality.

Revisiting the old Emily with the eyes of the new Emily Carol is what I need to do to further heal.

Boy howdy. I've put this off. I thought it was out of laziness, but I think it may have also been out of fear of the fatigue and sickness that rereading my entries may coax me into. Perhaps that is something that will be good for me to face, however.

9/30/2020

Psychiatric limbo leaves me manifesting realities. Psychotic episodes unlike the ones I have become used to. Years of misdiagnoses and hate towards a lack of progress towards a legitimate and successful treatment. Slice me, laugh, sway and dance, become your divine.

Undated 2020 reflections:

Relief warms me and I relax. I have a plan.

A confession. Psychiatric honesty. A revelation. A misdiagnosis. Not bipolar. More likely borderline. It makes sense, and I certainly will benefit from the medication adjustments I need. Antipsychotics definitely make a difference, and, boy howdy, I need that. My world is melting and swirling, and then it wisps away, leaving nothing but the illusion of me.

I'm grateful that my mom scheduled a phone appointment with my psychiatrist. (I forget how concerning my habits and social media posts can be to those on the outside.) My reality is frustrating and lovely and disgusting and enlightening and infuriating and beautiful. I am ill and I am in danger, and I know that, but I am trapped, and I am raging and my words race through the phone and I am relieved.

My psychiatrist is proud of me for being honest (I must admit, there are several omissions, but we all know that being entirely honest may end with our being too out of control. And I'd like to maintain the little control I have). She says that most patients do not open up as much as I did. They fear what I have, I'm sure. Being stolen. But I've already decided that I needed extensive help, so I don't care anymore, and I figure, "Oh hey, she's a psychiatrist, and I'm her patient, and she went through all this school to do this, and so I'll let her do her job, because, geez, psychotic symptoms probably don't shock her. Since this is her profession."

I received her notes a few days later. They were written as I rambled and were not grammatically correct and have spelling errors. I briefly edited them to make them more coherent:

"Mother made appointment because she is worried about Emily's mental instability. Emily states she is feeling overwhelmed, and has increased anxiety and depression. Reports constant dissociation: "in a dream state and separated from reality." Just sits or stands, non-responsive, and it is affecting work. Having about 5 mood swings daily. When she is in a good mood, any small thing can trigger anger, depression, and self-harm. Cutting on legs and arms, and though not too deep, worries it will get out of control. Then plays with blood, puts on face, and makes artwork which makes her happy. Tries to dance for a couple of hours or do artwork to help. Afraid how far she will take her negative thoughts, including suicidal ideation. Thinks about jumping off the pier or driving off a cliff. Clarified that she would not act on this and is not suicidal. Has been going on for a long time, though it's difficult to talk about and is getting worse.

Had ongoing vivid dreams which continue in dream-like state after waking in the morning. Sketches and writes notes about her dreams, which she enjoys. Reports auditory hallucinations, hears music like on a radio next to her, sometimes sees spiders across the floor, sometimes sees something out of the corner of her eye. Hallucinations/delusions do not bother her; she is used to them. Rarely hears voices– last time was before her hospitalization for 5150. Worries people are mad at her, like she's a problem and annoying to others. Doesn't want to hang out with people because she feels they pity her. So she self-isolates. Self-sabotages– not eating. Did not start therapy after last visit. Denies paranoia. Ongoing difficulty falling asleep, takes alprazolam, sleeps about 5-12 hours, depending if she needs to work. Patient was cooperative and polite. Speech was coherent and relevant. Mood was WNL, affect congruent to mood. Patient denies homicidal ideations, no psychotic symptoms. Alert and oriented x 4, cognitive functions are within normal limits.

Emily is the most expressive today about her symptoms she has ever been with me and she reports the same with her mother. Rambling thoughts for 40 minutes about dreams, dissociation, dancing, using blood for art, aripiprazole or paliperidone. Genesight reviewed. Declines starting, wants to start when she is inpatient. I do support voluntary inpatient care since she is not suicidal, recommend [an inpatient program] after she is tested and cleared for COVID-19. Called mother and updated her with Emily's consent. She will pick up note, Genesight, med list for collaboration of care. I will add Emily on to my schedule for f/u appointment after inpatient discharge."

Okay. So.

Her notes mostly sum up my overall issues. However! There are some things not recorded the way I meant them, and some details and truths I left out.

The dancing does not feel like a choice. I am compelled to dance. It does help in its own way, but it is not something I think of as voluntary. It can go on for hours and I switch the style of music and let the mood of the songs fuel me and I feel everything inside and I can't stop the emotions or the movements. Songs of rage, remorse, fear, sadness, peace, etc...they are in control. I lose myself in them. I can't come back until they say it's okay.

After the dancing I am in a state of euphoria. It's vibrant and pulsating. I am excited and overwhelmed, and that is when I merrily self-harm and, often, create art with my blood.

I am sated. It's orgasmic. I laugh and tell myself stories and jokes as I clean up. Some don't make any sense, but at this point, it'd be unusual if they all did.

And, holy fuck, I am definitely suicidal. I've been suicidal since I was twelve. The ideation is always there, and my craving is not always taking the reins, but it's not unusual for me to hold up a blade to my wrist and imagine pressing it into my skin. It's calming and sometimes helps me sleep. But falling asleep holding a blade isn't safe for my cats.

"Cooperative and polite" is a magical description that should be more unsettling than comforting. I'm struggling so much and am rarely grounded, but I'm putting on quite the performance.

I am going back into inpatient, and I will get my correct diagnosis, and I will be treated, and I will learn how to adapt my behavior.

Nah.

The promise of help laughs and dissolves into the popcorn ceiling of my Fresno bedroom. None of the promised inpatient housing. Calling around, and no other places open their arms either. I guess I can waltz into the ER and be 5150'd and sent to a holding ward until they ship me off to some holding unit that pretends to be something other than an extension of my ever-increasing, and rather humiliating, devastating, and infuriating psychiatric limbo.

Maybe I can find a place in SLO that will take me?

No.

In the meantime I can find a psychotherapist and have multiple sessions a week until I find somewhere to take me. Please?

No. Not that either.

Insurance and networks and policies drop kick me and I fall and am absorbed into the Earth, and my vision is fading and my breath is shallow, and I hear the life above me continue as I sink.

So, over one month later, I drink my coffee, listen to my classical music playlist, and lament on my misfortune. I'm dramatic.

Leave me to my melancholy!

Oh, and my insurance won't cover the antipsychotic my psychiatrist wants to start because they don't understand why it's necessary. I mean, okay, fuck you, too.

On the difficulty to convey my psychiatric situation as someone who internalizes most of my emotional responses:

I'm cooperative and polite.

I'm calm. I'm pleasant. I'm coherent.

My psychiatric turmoil doesn't often present itself on the outside, and so I may come across as balanced, calm, secure, "not in crisis or in severe need of treatment." To enter some programs, they send you through a series of (what feels like) tests. Are you sick enough? Are you still sick enough? Aaaand, are you sick enough? I made a habit of being outwardly reserved even while I'm screaming, raging, wailing, and breaking down completely on the inside. I'm cooperative and polite. I'm calm. Polite. Coherent. And I feel like it makes me less believable. I can describe what goes on inside me, but I don't change the inflection in my voice, grow hysterical, angry, etc... I feel it all. Oh, it's strong. It's invasive. But, talking to me, you'd think I was in control of everything. That perhaps I'm exaggerating. That perhaps I have more control over myself than I thought, and that I don't really need treatment.

It makes me disgusted by myself and the world. The entire time I'm answering questions and describing what I'm going through, a rage builds up because I know, I know they're not seeing or hearing my true reality. It's a struggle to make it through every day, every hour, every minute. But I feel a judgment from the public, doctors, and family that I am not that bad off, for I am managing to be quiet and calm, "polite and coherent." I want to burn the world and all the people who judge me. I want to slice my skin and bleed on everyone who has said or thought cruel things to and about me. I want to scream so loud that all ears bleed. Make all brains swell and make all feel like they'd rather drill into their skills and mash their brains than continue to feel the pain I grace them with. I want to stick my hand into the sharps disposal and decorate myself with the needles. Paint the walls and floors with the blood from my body I lovingly sliced. I want to stand and throw my chair at my "interviewer" and knock them to the ground, through the floor, into the Earth so they may be buried to suffocate, their final thoughts being that "she seemed so polite and coherent. Calm. Controlled."

I understand these thoughts are a part of my disorder, and I understand that, as professionals, they (should) understand that people manifest their disorders differently. However, I also know that the majority of people with Borderline, both real and in fictional media, react outwardly. Immediately. Triggered and BOOM! Screaming, crying, injuring themselves, injuring others. It makes me nauseous and petty. Jealous. Terrible, unjustified jealousy that so many portray characteristics so textbook that they are validated immediately. I'm not going to fake an external reaction. I've spent so long keeping it inside, learning how to keep my expression in between neutral and pleasant. Sometimes furrowing my brow. Letting some emotions slip without being too alarming. Even if the words I speak are disturbing, my countenance seems to be what is the deciding factor on whether or not I am stable. It's disgusting. So disgusting.

There can be a feeling of "competition" among the mentally ill to get some form of treatment. We don't mean to do it, and we don't want to. Beds are scarce, insurance is limiting, so only the most severe patients are admitted into programs. The others can go somewhere else. They'll send some referrals. And those referrals will send more referrals. It's a circle that will lead back to interviews. I'm concerned that if this continues, I may not be "cooperative and polite." A fantasy often runs through my mind when I think about the utter bullshit of this fucking mental health treatment nonsense; it runs through my mind as I speak with doctors: of my finally letting everything out. Wails of rage, my destroying everything around me, alternating between hurting myself and poisoning everyone with my words and violent physical reactions that have heated my blood for years. The disgust for myself and for others is what has kept my heart beating. I am my own God, and, like gods, I will do as I please. I will eventually reveal my fury and sorrow. And I will control my end. I will cause my end.

But, no.

Not me. I don't cry or yell. I'm cooperative and polite. I'm calm. I'm pleasant. I'm coherent. I'm just troubled, but maybe a session once a week with a psychotherapist (if I can ever find one that takes my insurance) will be sufficient. Just a couple of behaviors to whittle out of my system. Goddam fuckers. I've been self harming since I was twelve. And it was fucking compulsive as shit. The first time I cut myself, I was sitting on my bed doing homework, thinking about my day and my cruel peers. And then I dug my mechanical pencil into my left arm and dragged it up and down, up and down. Jagged lines of torn skin bleeding and swelling. It was euphoric. Spontaneous. I miss that freedom of compulsiveness. It's cruel, but I am jealous of those who react outwardly, right when the emotions hit. I just absorb it into myself until I'm in private. I feel almost cowardly. But it's how I trained myself, and until I am tipped over my edge, it will continue to be how I handle my emotional disturbances.

But the thought of being impulsive is so stimulating, and I feel the need to be so course through my body. An ache similar to the ache for sex. It simmers and builds as I internalize my desires instead of instantly acting on them. It spikes out of nowhere when I am "triggered" and it is painful and devastating and frightening to hold back.

But I do.

I'm cooperative and polite. I'm calm. I'm pleasant. I'm coherent.

Blood

I had a tendency to dance erratically in the dark. My emotions and the music drove me. My dancing built up a strange, yet euphoric tension, which I felt the need to slice out of me and paint with. My "paintings" remain as reminders of both the destruction and comfort I found through self-injury.

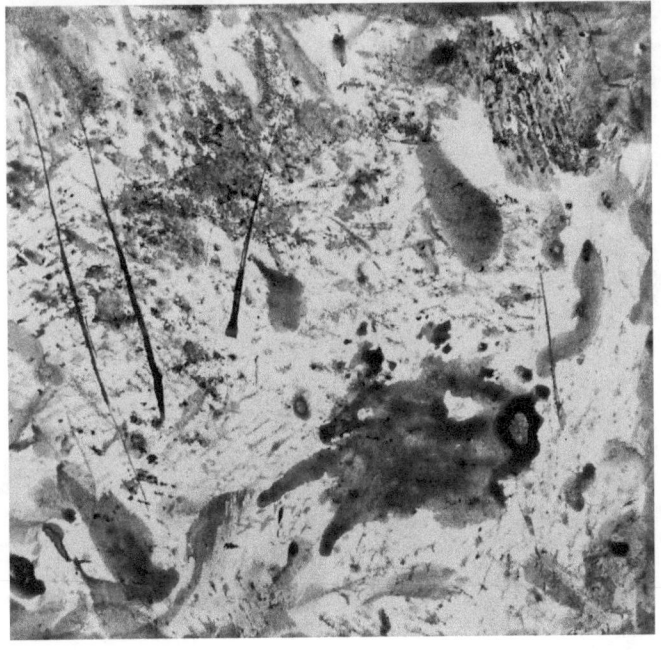

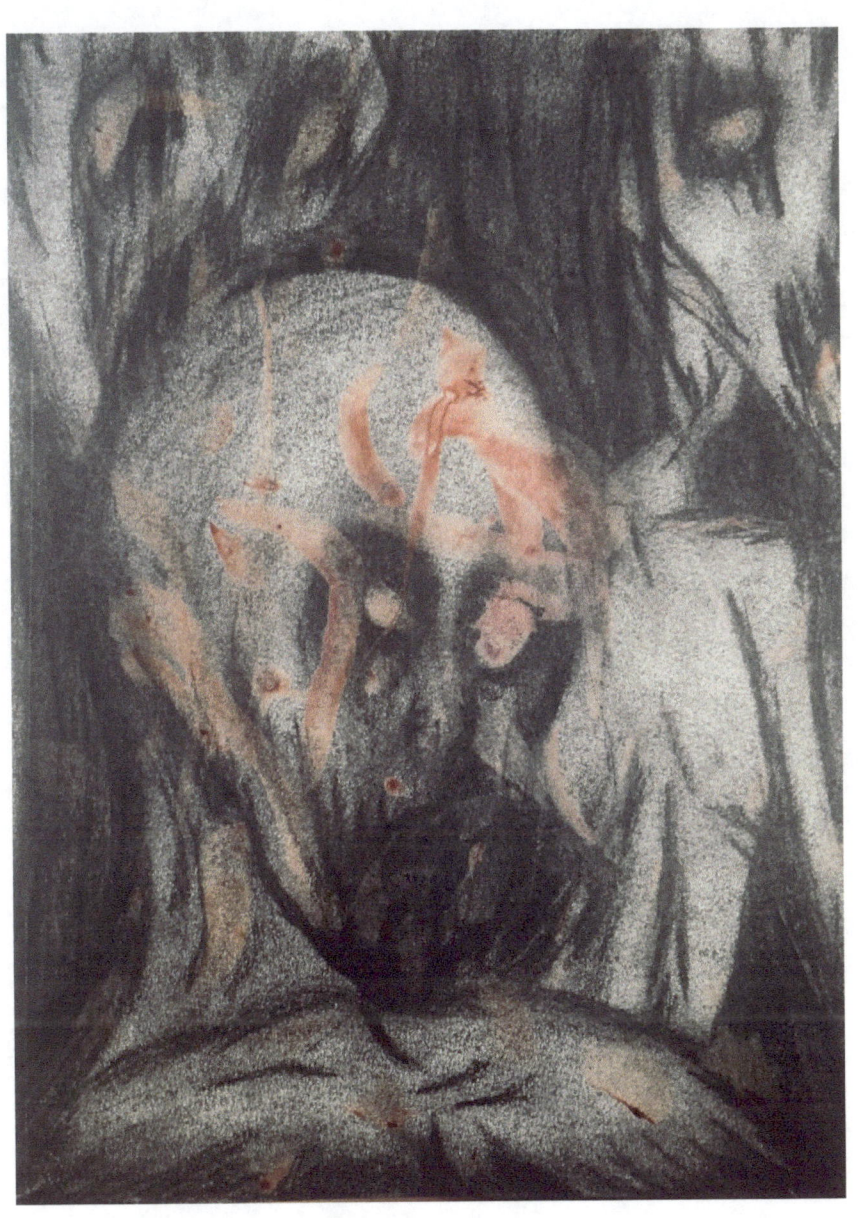

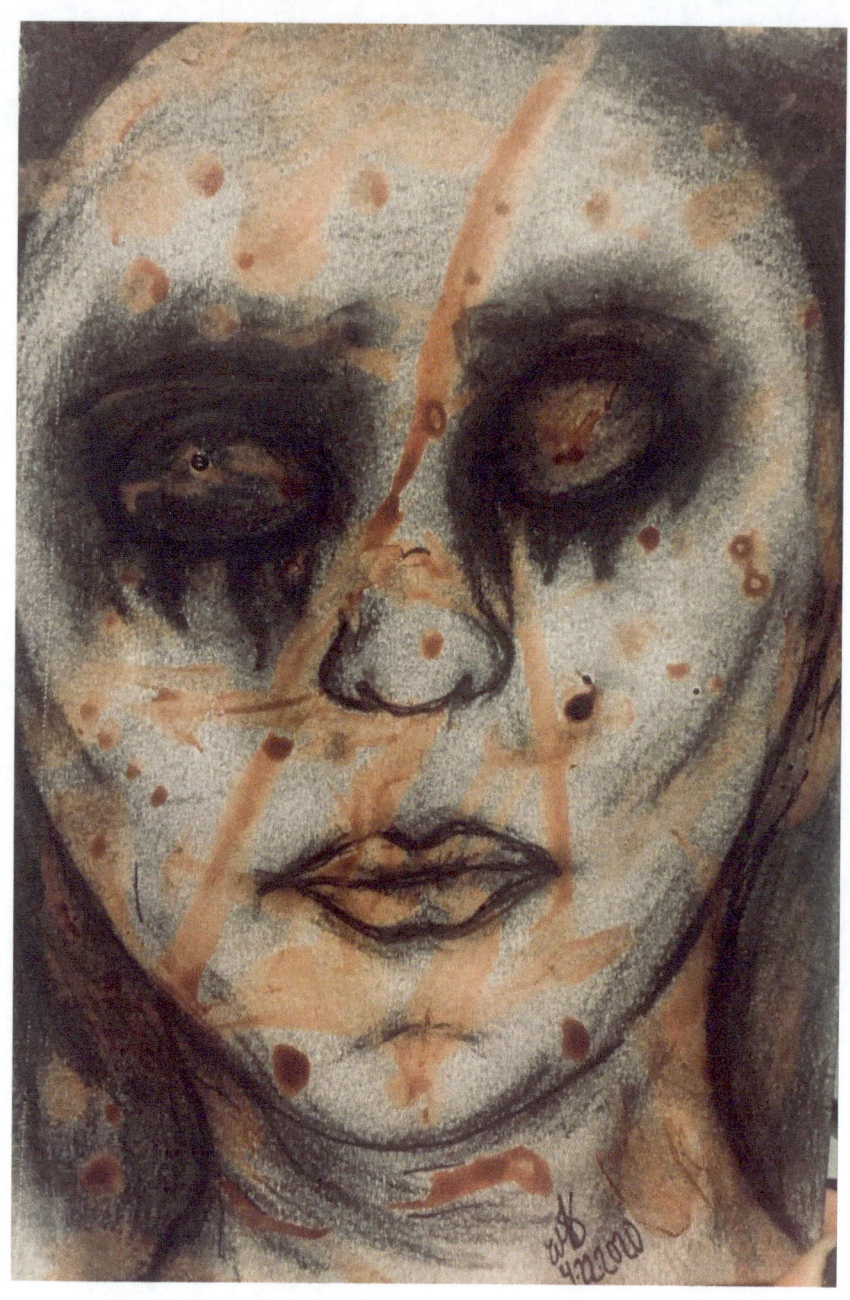

I Ruin

Every

thing

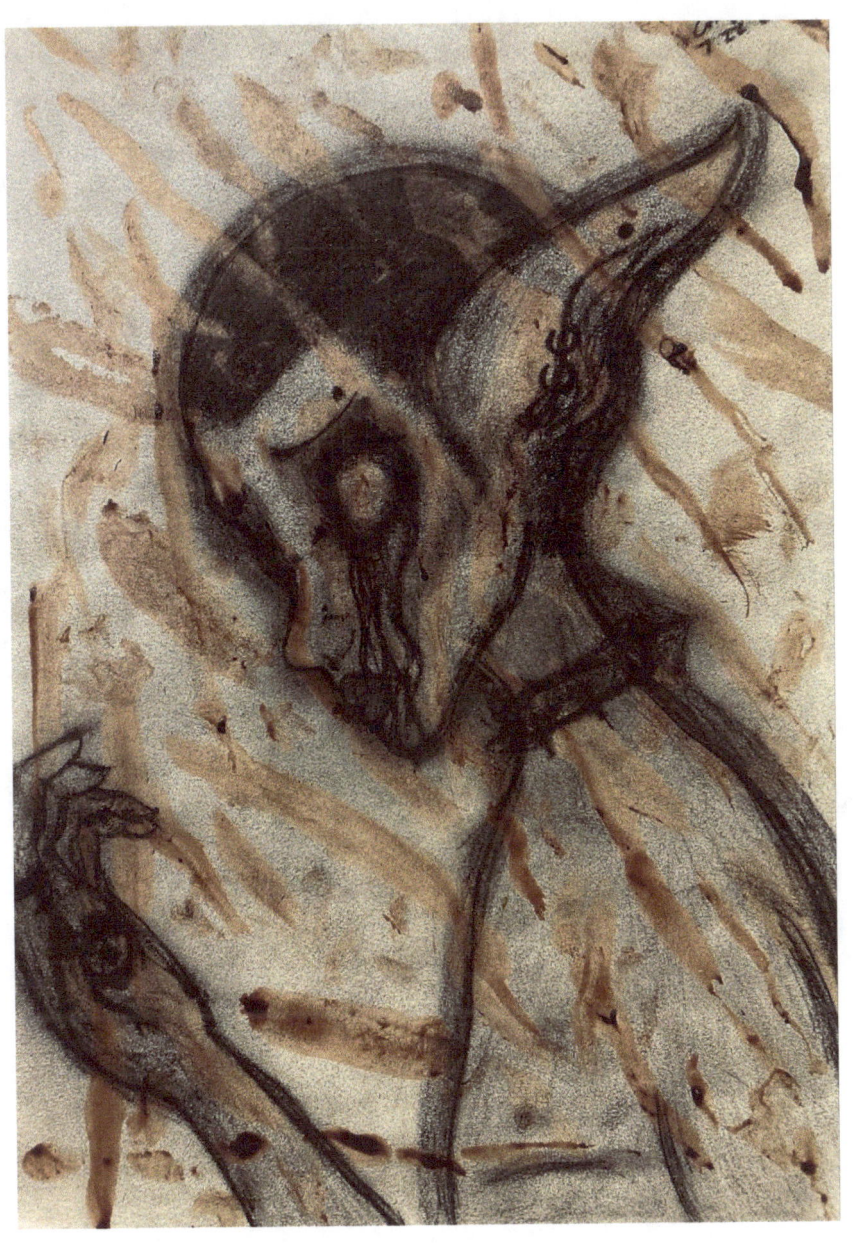

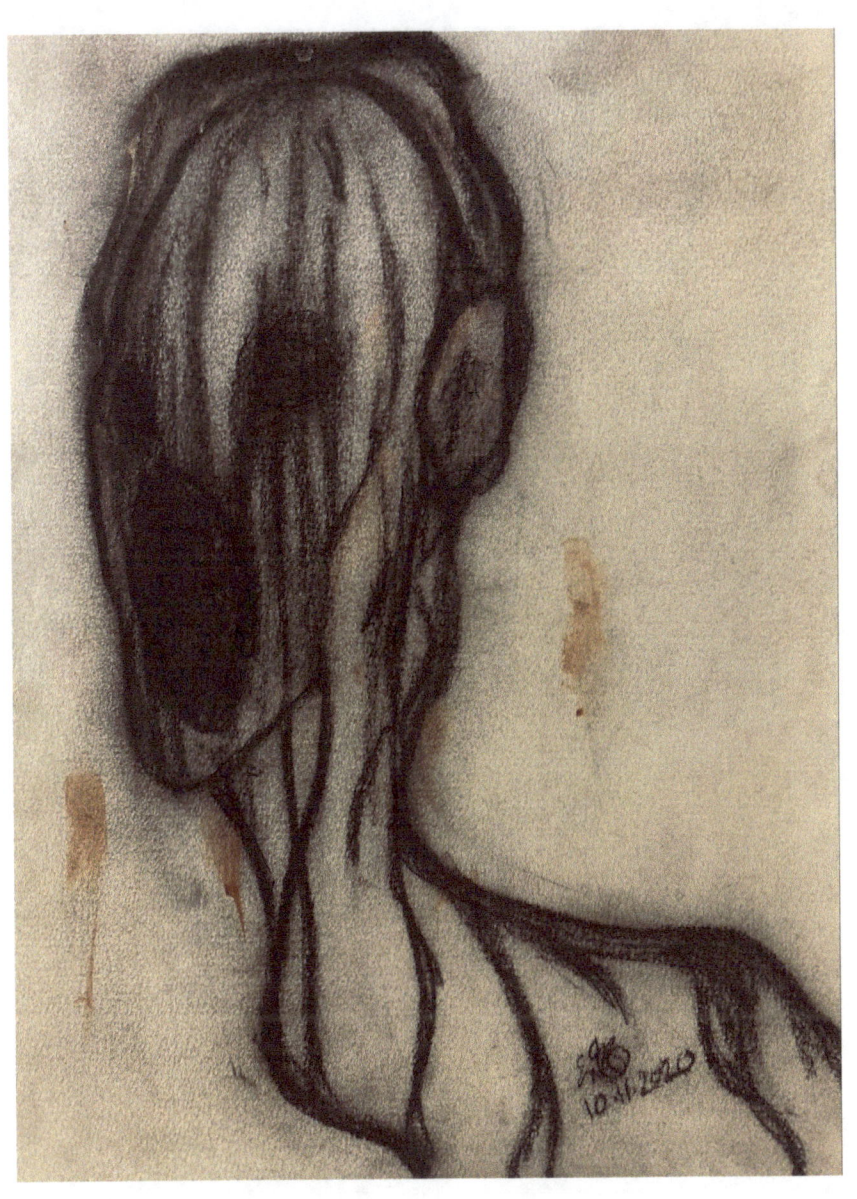

Magickal Morose

I embarrass myself with the cruelty I am capable of. I took my rage out on myself and tried to keep my poison in my own body, but my obvious instability did affect those around me. I am so sorry for the pain I have caused my loved ones.

I'm in love and have so many kind souls that support me wholeheartedly. I have found a great psychiatrist and have worked hard on regulating my emotional responses and behaviors. I still have so many habits to work on, but I have better accepted myself and acknowledge that those parts that caress me into starving myself or to binge or to slice my arms and use my blood as paint or to compulsively dance alone in the dark for hours, the parts that make me miserable to be around, that push people away, that make me cruel– all of those parts are still in me. I am all of those and more; we exist simultaneously. I have better autonomy, better control, now that I'm not suicidal, and I have gone the longest without wanting to kill myself since I was twelve.

The Emily Carol today is still the Emily Carol who imagined bug-like warriors to protect them. The same Emily Carol who loved horror films and wrote plays for their stuffed animals. The same Emily Carol who hated their body and regularly tried to destroy it. The Emily Carol who planned to die on December 8, 2011. I am all of them. My psychiatric void absorbed me for a decade, but I made it out– I occasionally drift into its hallways, but I can find myself out much easier now. I am better balanced and enjoy being happy with who I am. I'm healing.

I know this is not the end of my mental health journey, but I do believe that I am stronger and will be better able to face my struggles in less detrimental ways. I still have dismal moments, dismal days. My behaviors can be infuriating, and I can still be hard to understand. For now, however, I enjoy finally sitting down to write something other than a lament about how I never write anything, even though most of what I was lacking was my own initiative. I want to start to work on some of the fiction ideas I've been developing for several years. The plots and characters are there. Perhaps it's time to bring them to life. I think I'd also like to interact with my characters; decades of maladaptive daydreams make me a natural at involving myself with the lives of the fictional.

I'll need a disguise.

Magickal Morose seems like a dramatic enough name, and it certainly appeals to my love of the nauseatingly charming alliteration of Magickal Morose and the Meddlesome Melancholy.

There once was a strange one named Em
Who finally learned how to swim
They jumped in a well
Swam straight down to Hell
To unite both the joyful and grim

-(Revised) Limerick by Emily Carol (age 30)

Death and the Hermit

Another Death, Another Wander

Dead trees scatter the horizon. What I at first think are intense winds are actually other spirits' frantic searching– they move so quickly, and when they rush through and past me, their current states flash in my mind: chaos and confusion.

They're lost. Like me.

It's stagnant and desolate. The trees are either petrified or decayed. The ground isn't earth. It's just flat and grey.

When did I get here? I've been rushing among the trees just as the others. Constant. There is no time. Is this Death?

I sometimes forget I can die. But I now vaguely remember being human. And dying. I'm like static trying to form a thought. I feel weird. I want to rest and not get run through by these spirits. Each collision reveals their pasts to me; I'd rather remember my own.

It's a rule of the Treehouse..

A memory? It sounds familiar.

It's a rule of the Treehouse–

Treehouses shouldn't have rules.

– that it is a place of respite. You must leave your ill wills at the door. Any are welcome, and, as we are all Travelers here, no one is better than the other, no matter what forms we have or have not taken.

Forms. I've been many forms.

A place of refuge. To recharge. To rest. To reside. A hotel. A home.

A Treehouse?

The Treehouse.

Spirits whip around me, clipping me with their frights and unease. I'd certainly rather be in a treehouse right now.

And so I try to imagine that I am: I remember warmth. The smell of wood. Of books. The glow of candles, inviting and cozy.

Lights distract me. Where are they coming from? There are no stars, here, yet there they are: soft pink and yellow glimmers beyond the dull trees. I focus on them– they're crowded, muffled, but still there. I focus harder on them and realize they're coming from a tree.

I will myself closer. I can travel just as quickly as the others. I just need to decide where to go. I focus on the glow of the tree in the distance, and it speeds towards me, getting larger, luscious, warm, surrounded by the sounds of an Earthly night.

A light breeze, comforting, dances around me and I realize that the tree hasn't come to me– I've traveled to the tree.

Its branches erupt in light and its entirety expands and transforms into a massive oak tree. I hear the sound of a...knock? It sounds to be coming from inside the tree, so I put my ear to the trunk. It's warm. There's another knock. It startles me and I pull away to find myself staring at a door. I step further back.

The oak tree is now home to a massive treehouse.

There is another knock.

I step forward and gently push on the door. It opens.

The Treehouse

My favorite part of the Treehouse is its library. Many animal spirits also like to relax here. Perhaps they too find comfort in the library's warmth and the sound of pages turning. Some seem familiar, but I can't trust my memory. Dreams and memories overlap and feel the same. I close my book and stretch my toes in front of the fireplace. A fox stirs next to me, yawns, and stares up at me with content eyes.

Jodi, the Treehouse's librarian, sits down next to us and gives me an envelope. It's pink and has the name "Emily" written on it.

"Is this for me?"

"I handed it to you," Jodi replied.

"I was Emily, then?"

"You are Emily."

I try to open the envelope, but the paper doesn't tear.

Jodi stands. They stare at the fire and it grows bigger. Then they look down at me, smile, and instruct, "open it at the bottom of the stairs."

Alright. Jodi usually knows what they're talking about. And I'm curious.

I exit the library and take the stairs to the base of the Treehouse. Directly across from the stairs is the door I entered through...how long ago? I spin away from the door and look intently from the stairs to the envelope. Emily seems like such a common name. How many Emilys must there be? Maybe it isn't for me?

Jodi's dark eyes appear in my mind and I hear their voice repeat, "I handed it to you. You are Emily." They add, "Open it and take the left hand path."

I try again to open the envelope, and the paper actually tears. Left of what? There's only one staircase. I finish tearing the envelope, suddenly impatient. Inside is a paper. All it says is, "you're invited." That's it. No event. No name. Nothing but confusion and annoyance. I look away from the invitation and notice that there are now two staircases.

Oh.

I step towards the left staircase.

The Hermit

1993-2011

Going Left

The stairs spiral up a few floors before stopping at the end of a long hallway. Doors line the walls. Between each door is a portrait. I walk slowly and try to make out the faces in each, but the more I focus, the more the images blur. I look back at the stairs, thinking about returning to the library, but my wonder overpowers my hesitancy. I don't think I can die again, so what is the danger? Besides, something in me understands that satisfying my curiosity would certainly bring me back to where I need to be. Where I am safe, I think.

I glance at the invitation in my hands. This time it reads, "You're invited to Emily's Garden— a succulent, magickal paradise. Follow the stairs to remember the Hermit."

Remember the Hermit? The statement feels familiar. Is Emily's Garden mine or another Emily's? I only just remembered I was an Emily, and now I also need to remember a Hermit.

I feel an intense, invigorating energy erupt around me. Vibrations, both alarming and comforting, buzz and hum. I feel like I've felt this many times, but I rarely get to see what actually accompanies it.

"Hello, Hermit." The vibrating humming is also a voice— mesmerizing, powerful, layered. It is so familiar and ignites both warmth and a peaceful melancholy. I can't place the voice, but am sure that I've heard it many times before. I look around, but I know I won't see anyone. I don't think I often see the owner of that voice. Humans don't see a lot of things. And Emily was a human.

"Hermit," the voice repeats the name, this time sounding less surrounding and more localized— it seems to be coming from above me. I look up at the ceiling to see a marvelous, albeit startling, entity. Its form is long, and it stares with large, unblinking eyes. The more I focus on it, the more human its features become. A skeletal body appears over its original shadow. Floral and insect shapes travel along its bones as it becomes more and more three-dimensional.

The figure drops, encompassing me. I feel its hum run through me and its bones press around me, hugging me briefly. It's overwhelming, but the comfort it brings reminds me that I can trust it. I have always trusted it, I think. I feel like I have been waiting for this moment for many lives. Like I am tied to this energy but so rarely get to remember interacting with it.

The sound of bones clicking vibrates and the smell of earth permeates the hallway. I can feel the being reshaping itself— deciding on a final form to take before it fully manifests in front of me. It's at least thirteen feet tall— when did the ceiling get so high? It warps briefly as it settles into a form I can better understand, its skeleton becoming more and more human, as if it's trying to imitate something more familiar to me.

As I try to figure it out, it looks annoyed. The voice, now only originating from its physical being, is just as intense as ever, although more human– like a deep, warm alto; it blankets me. "I do not imitate anything, Hermit."

I remember now. I'm also the Hermit.

It continues. "I know you want to speak to me like this."

"I think we have spoken before, like this..."

"You have."

"And now?"

"Now we will speak again. Tell me, Hermit: what do you remember of yourself?"

"I'm a wandering spirit."

"Yes. And?"

"And I've been invited to a garden party, I think."

The intense buzzing vibrates abruptly in the back of my head. The figure grows taller– the ceiling rising with it. It unfurls massive, bony wings that creak and click and pop as they spread out, and several more eyes open among the ever-crawling and sprawling images on its skeleton. "You have begged to meet me in this way. I am here now. I will not act as an entertainer, so be present with me, Hermit, while you have my attention."

I try my best to remember, but although the energy of the entity is stirring some recognition, I can't remember a name for it.

"Because I have many names. I exist with all who may live. In many forms. Your memory is limited, but it will fill itself in if you let it. I don't owe you patience, so be quick. Look to your letter."

I look again at the paper still in my hand. It now reads, "Remember the Hermit as you walk with Death."

My own voices– different octaves, different languages, different species,– begin to mutter and shout and cry and laugh as Death widens its eyes which are now full of stars and planets. I gaze deeper into them to also see nebulas, promises of life. "Where you come from," Death's voice overlaps with mine.

The voices quiet until only one begins to recite, "In a year, 2011, Emily bled out on her bed. She longed to love and to be present with her imagination. As she grew older, however, others found offense in her eccentricities, her natural darkness. She continued to feel rejected. She drowned in her mind, suffocated by self-disgust. Another death, another end to a Hermit's life."

"So what do you remember, Hermit?" Death's and my former voice ask.

The hallway darkens and I feel myself freefall for a moment as candles appear around me, their wicks lighting. The floor returns, and the hallway is no more: there's only a landing and green, carpeted stairs. Death is not visible to me, but I feel its energy buzzing around my temple. It's encouraging. The candles follow me as I ascend the stairs.

The Birch Street House

There is a house I haunt. My favorite home. I am strong and curious there, my energy embedded into it— I remember playing with clay in my room, rolling the dough, flattening it into the shape of a cat and pressing it into my yellow walls. Pushing my art into existence, I merge my energy with the house's. Residents, past and future, dream of cat-shaped shadows, especially when I am upset.

I remember the friends I made after a trip to a neighbor's cabin: spirits of the land I met while exploring their wooded home. Ancient beings. Knowing.

I remember other friends, not from this planet. What I adoringly nicknamed, "My Trickies." What marvels! A flash of memory reminds me that I've known them throughout time. Play with them. Miss them, always. Those spirits from the dark, the most natural state.

Death reminds me, "This house is where you live when you begin to doubt. Your cosmic past fades and you begin to shape the present form. A form that is taunted."

"Yes. They started being cruel. Because I was violent, but gentle. A heart of sweet darkness— harmless, misunderstood."

"They fear differences and don't understand the significance of a shadow."

"I know that now. But it still got to me, didn't it?" I think of my bleeding wrists.

"Not always. You'll remember, Hermit."

The stairs continue but a glimmer of light distracts my gaze to the ceiling. What look like two chapel doors rattle a moment before disappearing, leaving an afterimage of spiders. I try to will the doors back, but, instead of the doors, Death's face manifests and it tells me, "That's not your current moment. Be present with your journey." The stairs begin to move, as if on a conveyor machine, going up, up, and up on their own.

I let them guide me to another hallway. This one is very short. The stairs end and there are about three feet of carpet. Its abrupt dead end is decorated with a painting of two pine trees. "These trees are from my elementary school. I used to chew on their needles. They thought it was cute."

"You also scratched the kids," a cheerful voice reminds me. It's one of my Tricky friends.

"Animals scratch when they play! I didn't mean harm. I forget how to properly human more than I'd like to admit."

"Oh, you admit it, complain complain complain about it, lament and curse it," it corrects. "It's okay, though."

"Not to my peers and their parents."

"No. They say you worship the devil."

"Which devil?"

"Whichever they believe in. They say you're poisoned by the dark."

"They'll say anything to make themselves seem more worthy of peace." I'm remembering. "Besides, I like the dark."

Another Tricky voice reminds me, "There is heart in darkness." I smile as I remember dancing with spirits as a form of grounding myself: music of the Earth connecting me to emotions while empowering me to reach out to those who experience physics differently.

Trickies laugh and say, "You mix physics and mysticism. Your kind sometimes call that 'crazy.'"

"Crazy or real, it strengthens me and helps me to be and do better. I prefer to welcome the overlap, no matter how contradicting it may be to those outside of my mind."

"But remember their fear? Witchcraft confuses and frightens them. Makes them dangerous towards you. You are hung for it. Burned. Degraded. Exiled."

I gaze at the pine trees. One fades away and the other grows sickly and dry. I remember more. "The same people who demonize me don't ever try to understand the pentagram or the pentacle. The elements. They fear the unknown and are uncomfortable being uncomfortable during the learning process. Fear is too often a deterrent. But it's a part of learning. A necessary unease. It can be so exciting if you allow it to be and grow confident with it. Delicious. Exhilarating. Do not let it hold you back. Rather, let it help guide you. Information is important to spiritual success. After all, curiosity may kill the cat, but satisfaction always brings it back. Again and again and again..."

The painting burns, the embers dissipating until only a charred wall remains. I lift my arm and feel for a slim rope. I find it and pull down a folded, wooden ladder. Just like the attic ladder from the Birch Street House. I climb up and up and up...

A Fox in the Snow

I'm nearing the top of the ladder and my body feels different. Snow flurries flutter down from the attic. As my hands reach over the last step, they turn into paws. I finish up the ladder. I'm in a field of snow. It feels so familiar under my four legs.

I am a fox. The snow cools my paws. It's refreshing. I prance gleefully through a snow-filled meadow and into nearby woods. Death follows above me, and I am assured that I am safe. I feel familiar energies join us as I wander, mesmerized by the nature surrounding me. I like the woods. And it seems many creatures, from Earth and other places, also find solace in the woods.

"But remember to not lose yourself in them. Don't be bullied. Don't be manipulated," a Tricky says lovingly.

"Says the Tricky."

"A name we didn't choose."

"That's fair. I do like to invite chaos into me. Some of it is beneficial, but some is also entirely unnecessary. It hurts me."

"It does," a Tricky confirms. "But from it you learn to protect yourself and how to honor entities without allowing them to overtake you."

"I should still be careful. Otherwise I get stuck, stagnate, and forget how to feel. I make the arguable mistake of trying to befriend everything, but some things don't need to be a friend— some are not capable or have no interest, and it is unfair to demand their attention, but also unfair for them to manipulate my energies. I am aloof, too often. I can be quiet, and I enjoy regular solitude, but the intrusive shyness I have to regularly free myself from comes after it's a truth to others that I exist incorrectly. I retreat. I turn back to the shadows, but sometimes get lost in them."

"You find the right supports."

"From all forms. Although I have an aversion to humans. To my own empathy. I get lost in my own cruelty." I'm solemn and remember my unkind moments— actions and words that I regret from many lifetimes. "But, I also become strong again. Not *me*, me, maybe. Another one?" My fox brain stutters and I see flashes of familiar humans from multiple time periods and at varying ages.

"You see Hermits who survive," Death explains. Feathers flutter down from above, landing in the snow around me. "All are you, Hermit. A simultaneous existence."

"Yes, and I do become stronger and more ready to befriend, no matter the form or origin. I learn to be more careful. Learn discretion, caution, and restraint. I must remember, though, to never allow caution to become too intimately entwined with fear."

Trickies laugh. "You may find beauty, but you also hate, too. That can be fun, an experience...to be empty. It is easier." I again remember my cruelties. Forms of my more unpleasant selves overtake the previous Hermits.

"I have been terrible, I know. And I have a permanent sorrow in me. A guilt. Apologetic dreams. I think sometimes that I don't deserve peace. I am selfish and desire forgiveness, but I have caused overwhelming degrees of pain— I get lost in the memory of them. I don't deserve these woods; I deserve the grey, petrified trees among other lost spirits."

Death interrupts, "Hermit, if you're reflecting, apologizing, learning, then you need now only forgive yourself. Don't continue to make excuses for not improving yourself." Death's voice is deep and comforting as it asks, "How are you at this moment?"

"I think I'm a good being. But I am also cruel and deserve—"

Death interrupts again, "it's not about what you deserve; it's about what you learn."

I pause to carefully choose my words. "I've learned the importance of finding comfort in my humanity. It is difficult and tiresome, but that is a part of life. The more I try to distance myself from feelings, the easier it is for me to lose myself to frivolous, encompassing distractions. So I search for myself and allow myself to love deeply. That's when I'm my best. And through that, I find my own spirituality."

Death's energy surrounds me, hugging me close. The ground is now blanketed with feathers. I feel comforted. Relaxed. A blissful drowsiness takes over me.

I feel some of my Tricky friends begin to leave, off to other nooks and crannies and fields and woods. One teases, "They'll call you defiant. Rebellious. Evil. Possessed."

Another adds, "Yes, yes. For you honor and have fondness for those who have never been and never will be human."

162

I remember lessons I've learned. "You can learn how to honor and acknowledge entities without allowing them to control you. I also learn to protect myself from the projections against me from those humans who don't understand, who won't ever understand."

"They call you superstitious."

I laugh. "Oh, I'm not superstitious. I'm—"

A few Trickies mimic my voice as they finish my statement with me, "part of the superstition."

I nod confidently.

"Cute, cute," they laugh.

"Comforting." I think of Death's hugs. I wonder. "Death?"

"Hermit," Death replies, hugging me tight— the fierce energy securing and charging me. Despite the intensity, I feel more and more sleepy.

I yawn, closing my eyes tight; when I open them I am in a den on a bed of feathers. I remember my question: "do I offend you? When I kill others or myself?"

"I am indifferent to your corporeal decisions. Now, rest." I curl up and close my eyes. Death hums at me until I fall asleep. I am content.

What memories will I dream of?

Dream: Magnificent

Arianna Hernandez pulled me down a long sidewalk that led through the many gardens of my neighbor's property. The home belonged to Sallie Hart, an architect and philanthropist who held music gatherings for the neighborhood kids once in a while.

Arianna was the daughter of Sallie's accountant. We met in preschool. I was shy and often too nervous to approach others, but she decided she wanted to be my friend, and I'd have been a fool to let my anxieties keep me from her.

She'd sing at me, "It's yooouuu, Andreeeeew!" when I got dropped off in the morning.

She eventually invited me to one of Sallie's events, and we became good friends and ended up playing together often.

I didn't really understand what people meant by "crush" or "being sweet on a girl" until a few months ago. I started to wonder if Arianna had ever had a crush. I wanted to ask her– normally I would have– but the thought of that particular question made my stomach feel weird, so I never did. I didn't think she liked me "in that way" as I've heard people describe it, but I was confident that she genuinely liked me as a friend, which was what was most important. I wondered how we'd grow up. If we'd ever fight. Grow apart...

We made it to the other kids, their parents, and Sallie. We played and listened to music and ate delicious sandwiches and drank tea– Sallie never liked for us to leave hungry or thirsty.

When it was over, we began our walk home. We took the East garden to exit the property. There was a side gate that led to a beautiful hillside. As we walked, Arianna spread her arms wide, inviting the breeze to dance around her. "Isn't this magnificent?" She asked.

I smiled, feeling my heart swell. I replied, "Magnificent."

Dream: A Welcome Attachment

I rented a room in a haunted house. I tried to communicate with the spirit– he manifested the most in my bedroom since I was the most open to him; everyone else either disregarded or was scared of him.

One night, while in the dining room, I felt him struggle to manifest. I called out to and willed him to me, which helped him to come closer and appear.

I felt him approach, and then I saw a brief fluctuation in the light that surrounded his spirit. I was glad to finally be so close to him, and I could tell that he felt the same. I grabbed what I knew was the location of where his hand would be, and, as I did so, I willed more energy towards him until he appeared almost wholly human, although still a little "floaty" and mildly transparent. His hand was in mine, and we were happy.

It was overwhelming how warm we both felt from finally being together. He became more solid and we hugged tightly.

We talked all night.

There was frequent chaos in the home, but the ghost and I found solace and comfort in one another, and, when I moved out, I took him with me.

Dream: Eden

The original Eden Rivera wanted to spend more time looking at the stars, so we made a deal: she passed away shortly after her birth, and I jumped into her body.

Human form was new to me, and I felt constricted, but I was warm and felt an immediate bond with my mother, who was quite relieved when I finally cried.

Some days, my memories were hazy and I knew nothing other than my human life. The instincts took over and overwhelmed– being a baby, a toddler, a child– dealing with adolescence, puberty; sometimes I understood why the original Eden did not want to go to Earth.

Dream: Keys

My siblings and I lived in a city that was kept inside a giant dome. The corrupt government threatened many, but it was hard to escape the chaos. We were scrambling about– my brother disappeared entirely. I did not get out. Officials often lined us up and drilled us on "new history" and made sure we knew that they had complete control.

One day, while lined up, a guy in the row parallel to mine and I managed to escape out of the dome and found ourselves in an abandoned city. Apparently, if we stuck pencils into tiny holes in some of the buildings, secret doors opened and we could collect these weird looking metal things about an inch and a half long. I only collected three. I met up with some others who had escaped and who also collected the metal "keys." I died before ever realizing what the keys were for, but I let the guy I'd escaped with keep mine. Perhaps he found use for them.

Dream: The Set

I was in a play and the theatre was haunted. The set on the stage was built and decorated like a room in a mansion our director grew up in that had recently been torn down. If we walked onstage at a certain time of day, it transformed from a set into the real mansion it was designed after—a ghost of a memory turned tangible.

The other kids and I would play around on it outside of rehearsal because sometimes the real mansion's past occupants appeared when their room did, and they were fun to talk to. They were convinced we were the ghosts, despite our telling them we weren't. However, we never left the room when it became the real mansion because we were scared of becoming trapped.

If we went into the theater's upstairs bathroom, spirits in them rushed us and took over our bodies. I freaked out because my body was possessed during a rehearsal break, and I needed to find a way to switch us back to normal by opening night.

Dream: Jodi

Some monsters hid under beds.

We didn't grab ankles or bite fingers. Well, usually: there were always some ornery ones who enjoyed unsettling humans, but I didn't really interact with them. They were usually really loud and aggressive and I just didn't need that kind of energy in my life. Besides, we were normally very solitary creatures, and it wasn't uncommon to have limited friends. The more attention we attracted to ourselves, the less likely we were to get a restful night's sleep.

We dreamed when humans dreamed. The energy of dreams refueled us just as sleep did for humans, and sleeping directly under beds allowed us better access to the dreaming mind. I just cozied up once the human settled down and hopped into their subconscious, during which I turned transparent so as to not be disturbed should a human's companion glance under the bed. I rarely interfered with people's dreams. We weren't supposed to; that'd just tarnish the dream...overcook it and remove all the nutrients. Also, the more we interacted, the more fatigue we caused the human. And the majority of us depended on humans and didn't wish to harm them. Besides, I enjoyed not being in my own mind, and I relished giving up control at night, for my thoughts grew tiresome very quickly.

I moved around when I was very young, never staying under the same bed more than a few nights in a row. However, I did have my preferences. Some minds were empty, and provided rather mundane scenery and very little energy to feed off of. Others were too overwhelming. Like trying to cross a busy road while sirens blared and lights flashed— just too much.

I was about seven years old in human years when I first slept under Jodi's bed. I was tired and overstimulated from my day, and their window was propped open with no screen to have to push out and wrestle back in.

It was easy to sneak in during dinner. I waited in the corner of the room where I could still enjoy the evening's breeze and meditated myself into transparency.

Jodi's parents tucked them in not much later; however, upon their door closing, they sat right back up and read for an hour. The streetlights must have illuminated their room adequately enough. Then they left the room for a few minutes, returned, and rearranged their stuffed animals. They sang to themself while they moved the toys, stopping to address one occasionally. Once they had reorganized, they settled down to sleep.

It was a good forty minutes before Jodi's breathing slowed and I knew they were asleep. I repositioned myself under their bed and quickly fell asleep myself.

Jodi's dreams were the most vivid I had ever visited. It wasn't the sensory overload that some dreaming minds created; it was extremely realistic. Sturdy. Developed.

Grounded.

And from so young a human. They looked around the age that I looked. Seven. Perhaps younger. They were a bit small.

I remained an observer and floated behind Jodi's dreamself as they wandered down their dream's busy city street, passed restaurants and inviting cafes full of enticing smells, chatter, and soft piano music. Tourist shops, bookstores, record stores, antique dealers...the street was full of them.

Jodi entered a tea parlor a few blocks worth of distance from where I'd entered the dream. It seemed this city they were in consisted of one long road instead of many intersecting blocks. It was also very "tall", with five or six floors to each building. They sat down and ordered a jasmine green tea. It smelled so delicious; I just had to mirror their sensations into myself. When they swallowed the tea, I also tasted the realistic dream's recreation. I felt my body warm and relaxed. Jodi and I both sighed.

I encouraged Jodi to take another sip. I normally didn't like to involve myself so directly, but the sensations in this dream were so wonderful that I could not help myself. It was strange, though, for Jodi did not sip right away. Usually when I willed the dreamer, they reacted immediately. No, Jodi just smiled, removed their hands from the cup entirely, and crossed their arms in their lap. They leaned over the table and slowly inhaled the steam. The aroma teased me and I encouraged, once again, a sip of tea. Jodi's right hand came from their lap, and their fingers gently curled around the tea cup's handle; they were still for a few more seconds, and then they slowly guided the porcelain to their lips. There was another pause before they finally took a long sip.

Dream: Escape to Shore

I almost fell asleep at the wheel and so decided to pull off at the nearest rest area. I used the restroom, got some drinks and snacks from the vending machines, returned to the car, and took a nap.

It was always night. I was always driving. But I didn't care. I was supposed to care about a lot of things, but I never did. And I got tired of people expecting me to.

I didn't like to interact with others. I found, lately, that they mostly overlooked me, which relieved me. Less smiling on my part that way. Smiling made my jaw hurt.

I rubbed my jaw– painless. I hadn't smiled in a while.

I woke up and decided to use the restroom again before continuing on my way, but, after exiting the stall, I found myself in an empty hallway. I followed it and ended up in the back of a line. I waited until I got close enough to the front to realize that it was a line to see a movie. I paid the three dollar admission and entered a dark room. It was empty of other people and only had one chair. I sat and looked at the screen. All it showed was a silent snowstorm.

Hours passed and, eventually, audio came through. It was just murmuring, muffled and sleepy: "The pain we've known. It echoes. Everlasting. Our ways have been shown. Forever. Clouds are gone. No. Or dawn. The breeze. Until the sky's divided. Good night. Good night. Close the mind. Escape to shore. Good night. Goodbye. Gone to fly. Until morn."

The lights turned on and I stood and exited the theater. There was no rest stop anymore, no car, so I continued my journey on foot. I was by a bay and noticed a wooden bridge that extended over the water and disappeared into fog. I walked over and stepped onto it.

Dream: Of Math and Murder

My math teacher was angry because I needed to make up a test I had been absent for. Unfortunately, there was a deadly mist that was rolling over my school, so I had to move to a different location to take it.

The sky was dark. It was hard to find a place where I could see what I was doing, so my teacher took me to a tent, handed me a lantern, and told me to work right outside but to never enter. As I was taking my test, two people ran over and pulled me into the tent with them.

Once inside, time shifted and we were in the bodies from our past lives. We had to relive when we all killed each other; after, as dead bodies, we stood up and embraced each other, and then we dissolved and I awoke lying inside an empty tent, in my current body, and with an incomplete math test.

I got an F.

Dream: Charlotte

My spirit hovered over a young girl, maybe aged twelve or thirteen. She had brown hair and blue eyes.

An old, dark blue car stopped next to her. The driver, a woman about in her late thirties, rolled down the window. She asked, "Charlotte?"

"Yes?" Charlotte answered.

"I'm Julia's mom. Remember? I ran the art program last year for yours and Julia's class?"

Charlotte remembered, then, the freckles and orange hair. The backseat window rolled down. Julia waved.

"Please, let me give you a ride. It's too hot for you to be outside."

Charlotte shook her head. "My mom will be here soon. But if you don't mind, I'd like to sit in the car while I wait. Some air conditioning would be nice."

Julia's mother nodded and Julia opened her door and scooted to the other side of the seat to let Charlotte in.

Julia leaned over and whispered, "I know Edgar. He told me you created him." Charlotte didn't respond; her mouth felt dry and her heart pounded.

"I'm going to go park so we won't block traffic," Julia's mother said. She did a sharp turn. A light up yo-yo rolled out from under Julia's chair. There was a flamingo sticker on it; its string was pink. Julia ignored the yo-yo and reached into the pocket on the back of the seat in front of her and pulled out some napkins and old mail. She continued to dig around, focused, and then smiled as she pulled out a small zip-lock bag full of coins.

Charlotte said, "Coins...?"

Julia said, "Edgar."

"But how? I took care of that years ago!"

Julia had a sad expression on her face. She stayed silent.

Julia's mom said, "Julia! Don't scare Charlotte with your games. You're too old for that."

Charlotte took the bag of coins from Julia and held it close.

Dream: Squabbling Entities

I was arguing with another spirit.

I was so tired of being walked over and degraded, my energies used up. I had freed them centuries ago and they never treated me decently. Always taking and taking. They threatened to influence someone to banish me somewhere. I was livid. I replied to their threat, "you came out of a stained glass window. Essentially could have shattered you...made your bits all pokey and abstract, but I stuck you together with spit. I helped you out of that prison, politely, gently, held your hand, made sure you weren't hurt in the process. Don't you dare complain to me and put me down, or I will shove you, impolitely, back into a window. Then I'll dive through it, head first, to shatter you. I'll scatter you around junkyards all over this world. You'll never get put back together, you thick egg. You'll just watch the clouds from amongst all the other garbage."

Dream: Quest for The Maritime Forest

My sister, my friends, and I were traveling by way of a small, flying boat; we were the ones who powered it. It was simple and didn't have wings. Some flight boats had wings, but they were too expensive.

We all had some sort of power. Mine was momentary levitation. I could use it to catch a fall or lift myself up to grab something from a high cabinet, but it would not be strong or consistent enough to allow me to fly. My sister could create things by singing about them, but they survived anywhere between a couple minutes to several centuries; she could not determine their longevity, or lack thereof, ahead of time. We'd likely all develop better control and strength with age, but we were adolescents at the time. There was a young boy, Manuel, around age nine, who could come back to life. We had a feeling there were limits to his "lives" and tried to keep him from jumping off of high walls for fun.

We could all channel our power to the "boat" to make it fly. The more of us on board, the smoother the sailing went. If we all fell asleep, the boat would crash, but that was more-so due to our age and inexperience with magick. When I tried to fly it alone, it tipped and wobbled; it did not want to move in the correct direction. We landed in an ocean town at a temporary hub that looked like the top floor of an abandoned parking garage.

There were three stairwells. One stairwell led down to a stage theater. One led to a fast food restaurant. One led to a hostel that had a pool and regular movie nights. The actors for the theater and the employees at the fast food joint all lived there. Manuel kept jumping off of the garage.

At some point, I found dozens of racks of clothes– a "community closet". I picked out a dark green dress to take. One item per soul only, or we got penalized, I think. At some point, we all got separated, and I needed to power the boat on my own, which was difficult. It was hard to avoid telephone wires and traffic; it did not want to fly high enough.

I flew my boat over a part of the ocean that ran into the forest. I turned around, parked, and entered the forest on foot. A river of ocean water ran through it and there were stairs leading down into it from multiple areas and different varieties: wooden, steel, gold, pewter, and some even carpeted.

The further into the forest I went, the more calm and more clear the waters became.

Dream: The Green Man

I had a roommate who was sad because her ex couldn't get over the death of his younger brother who had been decapitated in a motorcycle accident. Every evening, he went to his brother's grave at the school cemetery, and every night, a green fog descended from a nearby hill. He tried to follow it, but it always disappeared once he got close. My roommate tried to get him to move on, but he got annoyed with her. Out of anger, she gave me a vase that her ex said his brother bought the day before he died.

I decided to take the vase to the grave. It felt like the right thing to do. I started on my way to the cemetery, but got lost in the green fog. I heard a voice say that if I passed a test, I would win the brother's soul and could bring him back to life.

A door appeared in the ground and opened to a set of stairs. I took them to a long hallway which I followed until I came across a doorman standing next to a cabinet. He opened the door and I crawled through it and into a small room.

Another girl appeared, claiming to want the soul– she was unnaturally infatuated with the dead brother, but, since she was not human, if she won, she would take his soul away instead of returning it to his Earthly body. We had to go through an obstacle course which had hidden paths and staircases and traps. We had to find the right way– even if it meant jumping into a hole under a couch...we were encouraged to "follow our instincts". I was far behind the other girl most of the way, but eventually caught up to her.

The Green Man appeared. He apparently collected coveted souls to keep himself alive. However, he was quite friendly. I'm not exactly sure what happened during the final part of the race, but the green man took the vase from me. He jumped onto a platform and held up the vase, which then emitted a green light and a floating green bracelet. A whirling hole opened above us and pushed wind down on us. The girl fell after only a few moments. I jumped onto the platform as it rose higher. The wind pushed down hard on me, and the hole in the roof was getting wider, and the bracelet was getting brighter. I climbed onto the platform and tried to grab the vase, but was blown down by the wind. I held onto the platform, demanding that I get the vase. I couldn't hold on well and was losing my grip.

The Green Man used one hand to keep me from falling. The vase was still in his other hand. After a while, I began to slip again, and he dropped and shattered the vase and pulled me up. He put the glowing green bracelet around my wrist and told me that the bracelet was what held the boy's soul.

The Green Man helped me back to the surface and then disappeared.

Dream: Adventures Through Space

I performed on a spaceship. We traveled to different planets, sometimes touring for years on end. I had a tendency to tell when beings wanted to escape their worlds, and it brought me joy to offer them safe boards on the ship.

I rescued a girl named Helen from Earth. She could create creatures, but she was forced to make them for governments. They were made to kill others and themselves. The ones who escaped their captors were still considered by humans as monsters, and many were killed out of fear. Helen could destroy them herself, but she didn't think it was right to make that decision for them— they had grown into sentient creatures who desired to thrive and not exist as throwaway weapons. Helen and her creatures happily joined our ship's crew.

If we couldn't enter a planet's atmosphere to dock, I sent a ladder down from space, transformed into a spider, climbed down, then found and guided people back. One spirit hid in a lamp for decades before I helped him out. He hadn't meant to stay there so long, but he forgot he wasn't a lamp. I broke the lamp, freed him, and we both climbed the ladder to the ship. He didn't stay on the ship; he darted off to a distant star. He said he'd been cold for far too long.

In another world I visited, there was a strange cave in an amusement park that a coworker and I got trapped in. In order to survive, we had to find "the Fruit Punch". There were signs for it, surprisingly, so we thought it could be part of an attraction. We managed to escape without any fruit punch, but a friend and I returned later to explore further. I became sick that time; my blood started to turn into Fruit Punch. My friend exclaimed, "we've found it!" After he said this, my blood returned to normal. The cave laughed at us when we left.

While on leave, I ventured back to Earth to visit my friend in Connecticut. Her house was a maze. We stayed there awhile, but then vacationed to different planets. On one of the planets, roller coasters were used as buses. Its moons had the same transit system; I could see tracks on their surfaces. We loved the thrill and it was much more affordable than a theme park.

Dream: Behind the Scenes

I followed my body from above.

I worked in a shop and liked a girl who worked in the opposite end of the mall. Sometimes, the mall would "glitch" and someone could find themself "behind the scenes" and see weird "people". They looked like humans, but they were out of focus and glitchy– a little robotic looking, and they swept the area to capture visitors who got stuck there. However, people didn't get stuck permanently when a glitch happened— just until another one happened again.

The "people" didn't walk; they slid and were more mannequin and cyborg-like. They'd sometimes throw the "captured" into the entryways of stores; once near, corrupted human entities pulled the humans in and trapped them, their bodies turning into a blend of thick vapor, bones, and human entrails.

When "behind the scenes" one had to stay in the hallways and not enter any stores or they may explode into ash. However, the "people" frequented the main pathways. My sister was there before me to try to create a written record of what was going on compared to what people said was going on, but her journals disappeared or turned blank. She eventually started to act oddly. She twitched and zoned out and then disappeared.

I thought maybe I could visit my crush and look into my sister's disappearance, but I got caught in a glitch and found myself "behind the scenes".

A woman in her mid-thirties with long, brown hair and blue eyes was taken by a "person." However, she was not thrown into a store, but was instead taken to an office. It was dimly lit by an office worker's computer screen. The worker sat at a cluttered desk in front of a computer. My sister's missing journals and other similar reports were piled up from so many attempts to try to record about "glitches" and "behind the scenes" and the "people." The employee calmly looked at the woman, but did not quit their work; they typed vigorously.

Cameras lined some areas "behind the scenes" and fed to monitors in the office which showed both versions of the mall side by side. Was there a button to press should the "glitch" bring any visitors? Was that effect purposeful or an accident that was abused in favor of the "people?"

The brown-haired woman locked herself in a small room to the side of the office. A phone rang for a while, and when she finally answered it– I saw that it was the office worker who called, but the woman did not know that– there was just a weird buzzing that somehow translated information into her mind: the employee gave her advice on how to escape. The brunette pushed a desk aside. There was a window in the wall near the floor. She crawled through it.

I think a big group was trying to get through the mall to investigate or escape from something. My mom was there, too, guided by my sister's journal. It was a small, red one, but the words blurred or disappeared whenever anyone tried to read them. I died after trying to decipher them for too long. I don't remember how or why I was still there in spirit to observe.

There was another "glitch" and a giant, dark fog rolled towards everyone, capturing and killing all who got caught in it, like when a human would get pulled into a store. There was a weird barrier to climb over that would lead out from "behind the scenes." My spirit was able to help lift people over the barrier, but some were left stuck on the other side and disappeared as the dark fog met the barrier.

The brown-haired woman returned home. I think she had been separated from her husband during a "glitch" at the mall. I knew she had been unhappy with him about something and regretted the way they parted. She was glad to have escaped.

I wanted to observe the office worker more, to perhaps learn more about "behind the scenes," but when I returned to their office, they had disappeared. I realized they likely weren't human anymore, either. They seemed so familiar. I hoped we'd meet again.

Home

I wake up, but am no longer in my feather-bedded den. I feel a soft malevolence– it's warm, cautious, as if it doesn't understand just how much it can frighten. Death's vibrations support me as I focus and try to see whatever entity has joined us. I am no longer a fox. I am human and am back on a stairway landing. I stand and start up the next flight of stairs. I can feel Death and the mysterious presence guiding me.

I am unsure of the stranger.

"It's just you," Death explains.

"That's not necessarily comforting," I reply, now better remembering versions of myself who were cruel, vicious, uncaring– desolate, inside and out.

"It's still just you," Death reminds.

I have no desire to reveal that darkness, so it remains invisible, only a feeling, a weight, an intensity that tugs at my limbs and makes me want to scratch my skin away from my bones.

"Just. You." Death's energy vanishes as I reach the top of the stairs.

I follow a hall to a bathroom. I look into the mirror. I feel odd. A panic rises in my throat. The presence is merging with me, and I begin to pull at my skin. Picking gently, slowly, at first. Getting bolder as my flesh peels more and more easily the longer I keep tugging. It feels like scratching an incessant itch. Like soothing a burn. Like biting into skin, teeth finding resistance before finally piercing– a satisfying breakthrough. I look back into the mirror, and my reflection sighs in relief: a bloody face, painted with an Earthly residue– a stain to remind me of my past mortalities.

"Oh, you," I say to myself. "I forget to reabsorb you, and I try to hate you, but I need you. You try to hate me, too, but you are me. You hate yourself, sometimes, just as I hate myself."

I'm confused. Angry. Merged once more with a part of myself I too regularly shun rather than try to understand or comfort. I touch the raw flesh of my face, delicately dancing the tips of my fingers on it. Then I press harder. And harder. I tear at the muscle and bone and veins, pull out my eyes and teeth. I feel my face come away.

I tear the rest of my body apart. My reflection disappears. The visible parts of me lie in a warm, pulsing heap of flesh and blood and bone on the floor. I push my energy forward and into the mirror.

Lost, Again; Again, Lost

I'm not sure what town I'm in. Or what time. Or what planet. My penance for my more cruel iterations: forever searching. For another me to kill. And when I finally come across the other me, when I'm finally about to put in my final blow, my body falls apart. Its pieces slip around the other me to rot and be absorbed into the ground. The other me forgets, my presence no more than a shadow of a stain and an odd daydream. Then I wake up in a body already walking towards the next town. Me again, just in another coordinate in space. On another rock. Revisiting places I've missed. Places we'd had the most fun.

We?

Oh, right. Him. We came from the same star, I think. Fragments from the same stone. We understand each other.

My current walk leaves me standing on the shore of a bay. It's calm. Foggy. There is a long, wooden dock that disappears into the mist. I step onto it. I walk and walk and walk. I expect to reach the end of the dock soon, but it just keeps going. It's okay; I'm enjoying the serenity. The quiet.

I hear steps approaching me. I continue forward and prepare to face another version of myself. I see a figure emerge at me from the fog, and I come face to face with Him. It figures we would overlap.

"You," I state flatly, but with a smile. He says nothing. I continue, "Did you kill me?" I don't remember how or when I died. It hadn't seemed important– but if anyone were to know anything about my most recent end, it'd be Him.

"No," he answers.

"Do you know who did?"

He looks annoyed, but I enjoy frustrating him. His lack of response answers for him. I move on to the more important question: "what's on the other side of the dock?"

"It's not a dock. It's a bridge."

Oh. Duh. I ask, "How long have you been on it?"

"I don't know. I tried to keep track of time, but quickly realized that was pointless."

"Did you run into other Yous?"

"Yes."

"Do you want to talk about them?"

"No."

"Okay." I step around him and turn. He's still facing away from me. "Do you want to come with me? Maybe we'll end up somewhere different than where you came from. Since I'll be there too, this time."

"You'd like me to go with you."

"Yes, please."

He turns and steps towards me.

We continue back the way he came from.

Ruthie's Roots

"Do you know why we're only running into other versions of "me" but not other "yous?"" I ask.

"Yes."

"Why?"

"I don't care about my others. There is no yearning for understanding, so I never interact with them. You do care. You care too much."

"I have to care this much in order to make up for how much you don't."

"That's unnecessary. You know that."

"It's a balance. You know that."

"You'd find balance without me."

"But I like you. I'd miss you terribly!"

"Then it's good that you died first."

"I know."

Ever since we came back from the dock– or bridge, I guess– he's been appearing by my side every time I re-manifest somewhere. He doesn't mind and I enjoy his company.

"Did you ever miss me?" I ask lightly.

"I missed your convenience."

"A willing, unattached play-thing that also helps pay the rent?"

"You got attached."

"Well, yeah. And that's why it's best that I died first. I'd care if you were gone, while you don't really care either way, so it worked out best for both of us in the end. No stress. All good."

He stays silent. He knows I'm talking more-so to myself than to him. He calls it my "verbal recalibration."

"I know you stress sometimes," he says.

"Yes," I admit.

"I can't."

"I know."

"You can never change me."

"Your consistent bitter indifference is what I most adore in you. If you were to change, you wouldn't be the you that I love. I know you can't reciprocate."

He lightly pats my upper back and says, "Look up."

I do so and see a long pull-string coming down from the clouds. The Attic, my mind wanders. I've pulled that string before. But it's too high up; neither of us can reach it. He again pats my back, firmly this time. I turn and he points to the string and then to himself. He crouches so I can sit on his shoulders. He stands and I am barely able to reach the string. I pull it and a wooden ladder begins to unfold from the sky.

He helps me off his shoulders and pulls down the rest of the ladder. I approach it, place my hands on it and feel him pat my back once more– a final, encouraging push. I begin to climb. The closer I get to the top, the colder it becomes. I step up into a snow-filled meadow. I turn and see that he is not behind me. The ladder is gone. I am alone.

"It's good I left first, again."

I wander, confused, cold, and stumble across a den. Inside, a fox sleeps on a bed of feathers. It's surrounded by a vibration that draws me closer. It's familiar. So is the fox. I am too tired to kill, to be mischievous. I decide to take a nap, instead. There's plenty of room on the feathers. The fox looks so peaceful, and the surrounding frequencies hum a promise of true rest. I lie down next to the fox and close my eyes.

Musical Episode: Creature Feature/Death Witch #9

I wake up in my yellow room. My soul feels heavy, the room claustrophobic, the energy phoney, and my emotions stifling. I place as many plushies as I can fit at the center of a blanket. My tears blind me and I struggle to gather the fabric into a sack and tie it to the end of a large stick. I have no more desire to live with humans. They are cruel and confusing.

I leave the Birch Street House with my plushies. I say goodbye to my cats and tell them they can visit me anytime at my new home in the woods.

I leave my stagnant city behind and begin my walk among the trees.

"The Hermit's Lament"

I love so deeply, but I do not love correctly
How I expose my heart's often misunderstood
Fun facts without emoting, non-verbally ecstatic
Dissociations versus dramatics: my imposing tendencies
The roots of who I am, my base, core characteristics
Are what people often cite as my lesser qualities
I try to follow human manners, rules, and regulations
But my resting state portrays indifference, and my heart bleeds harsh unease

Sometimes I feel like I exist incorrectly
When all I'm doing is trying to be me

Some of my Tricky friends join me. They take the forms of other animals. Some have extra body parts, some are just bones, some are in states of decay, some are just shadowy silhouettes; all are beautiful to me.

"In the Woods"

Love, oh love, the Ancient Ones
The wisdom in the woods

Rediscover my old loves
The Trickies in the woods

Inspirational aspirations of intensities
Unconditional, Un-reprehensible, Unadulterated Love

We play in the woods for a while.
The Trickies ask, "Do you prefer comfort or honesty?"
"What about the comfort *in* honesty? I'll take that."

"Masochist."

We roughhouse. Our noises attract another to us, and I recognize him. He recognizes me, too. We always appear in some way to each other. At least, I think, we try to. This body of his lives in the woods with his dogs. I invite him to join us. I introduce this Mountain Man, my Love, to my friends. They greet him joyfully and introduce themselves:

"Beloved Trickies"

We're here, we're there, we're everywhere
Under the steps, in corners, mirrors
We love to watch and follow near
Sincerely, Resident Trickies

(Oh, how I love my beloved Trickies!)

We dance and play. My Love fishes while I climb trees with my friends. We gather to rest by a lake.

"Want to be terrifying, today?" Trickies ask us.

"Sounds beautiful. I'm in." My Love passes on the offer. He leaves with his dogs to grab some snacks and drinks from his cabin.

While we wait for him, the Trickies teach me how to better startle people in the places I haunt. It's such wonderful fun!

I say, "Oh, it's so much nicer here with you all! Did you know, in the city, they expect us to act much the same?"

"Yes," one replies. "Truly horrendous."

"Truly boring," another adds.

Trickies and animals gather as I mimic those who ridicule me, "don't be so *offputting*, Emily. Be friendly! Smile! Look them in the eyes."

"Blah, blah, boo!" They chant and cheer and throw sticks and rocks and leaves and dirt and flowers into the air.

"If I'm not acting *their* normal, apparently I'm doing it wrong."

"Doing what wrong?"

"I don't know. But apparently it's wrong."

"What if they're doing it wrong?"

"They can't comprehend being anything less than perfect. That's why they bully. I may not be objectively right, but I do what's best for me."

"Offputting"

When I'm relaxed, happy, lost in thought, pleasantly daydreaming
I don't lock eyes and vocalize— that invokes negativity
I do acquiesce to workplace norms; in public I will appease
But sometimes when existing I'll do what's most functional for me

I know I can't go nonverbal, burrow hours in the dark— as much as I may dream

Even when I'm feeling my worst, I still understand there's a time and place for
everything
Maybe we should try to coexist with other behaviors
-which, although different, aren't meant to be rude
(or does approaching others' temperaments with respect apply to me but not to
you?)

My heart is full of peace and love, and so I am (un)surprised
That those who preach compassion find plenty faults in neurodivergent minds
There's (actually) quite a lot of us, so perhaps it'd be good to sometimes choose
To at least attempt to compromise with our mannerisms, too

I'm prone to overstimulation and so do what I can to keep some peace
Between my body and my mind— I won't simply cater to your unease
Consistently made to feel guilt and shame for who I am, naturally
No, I will partake in the self-care I need to thrive unapologetically

You demand we should adjust to you, yet whoddathoughtgoodgollygee
You're unable to realize our inherent mannerisms aren't abnormal to us (geez!)
Must we bow down to mold to you, oh so neurotypically
Our habits to be hidden and ostracized while yours roam dominant and free

When it comes to my ambiance and yours, comparatively
I find your abrasive extraversion (very) unappetizing
I'm healthier (saner) when I accept and adhere to my (carefully curated)
personal boundaries
If that's too offputting to you then, I dunno, just stay away from me
and don't you dare use my harmless countenance as a way to guilt trap and
demean

I'm overwhelmed, frenzied by my annoyance, and so I dance for a while— losing myself in emotions.

The Trickies say, "we like when you dance. So do the humans. The kids' spirits. They wonder why you dance so erratically, though."

"To ground," I answer. "To remind myself of how a human should work— should feel. It keeps me tuned into my emotions. I feel the drums, the bass...rhythms as heartbeats, connecting me to the Earth. I am sometimes begrudgingly human. I need to remind myself of how one works. Dancing helps with that."

"Let's keep dancing then!"

We dance and dance, but, again, as I enjoy myself, an uneasiness begins to grow within me. It's hard, sometimes. I get so frustrated, my natural state feeling, at times, a bit too unbalanced. The less confidence I have, the more uneasy I feel. The trees grow gray. The air grows stale.

I reach for my meds, but realize I didn't pack them.

Perhaps it is for the best; I don't trust the help they offer me, anyway.

"A Hesitance to Medicate"

You claim this anger puts me in danger
Decided that my life needs to be in safer hands
Your books have taught you, from all their experiences
A myriad of methods you don't even understand

Do you even have a clue
What your judgment puts me through?
Would you follow as they instruct you to
If the subject were not me but you?

You say I should amend
These thoughts that never end
Does your solution require more rituals
On which I must depend?
Why don't you explain again
How my life will not truly begin
Until I've deserted all I've learned to love
Deserted how I've learned to live

You ask to understand
So you can fix me
You ask to understand
So you can fix me?

How can I ever possibly find
A way to describe these worlds in my mind
Especially to the blind
To those who will never realize:
Real or imagined?
Both are bound to happen
Although they may seem as delusions, twinkling illusions
They're real to those who can see
Without them we could not be
They are our reality
Yet you dare to ask this of me?

You preach that, in time, with your professional guidance
My mind will clear and become a safer tool
These thoughts shall slow; I'll sleep peacefully at night
I can trade my wonder to become a blissful fool

Do you even have a clue
What your judgment puts me through?
Would you follow as they instruct you to

If the subject were not me but you?

I can see how you would think
How it shouldn't be so hard to choose
That I might as well put these to use
Rather than suffer from my own abuse
But after years of this devotion
To my mind's erratic emotions
I do fear that this practical plan
Will erase part of who I am

How can I ever possibly find
A way to describe these worlds in my mind
Especially to the blind
To those who will never realize:
Real or imagined?
Both are bound to happen
Although they may seem as delusions, twinkling illusions
They're real to those who can see
Without them we could not be
They are our reality
Yet you dare to ask this of me?

You ask to understand
So you can fix me
You say you understand
And that you can fix me
You ask to understand
So you can fix me
You say you understand
And that you can fix me?
By hiding away what makes me?
By stealing the pain that saves me?

How can I ever possibly find
A way to describe these worlds in my mind
Especially to the blind
To those who will never realize:
Real or imagined?
Both are bound to happen
Although they may seem as delusions, twinkling illusions
They're real to those who can see
Without them we could not be
They are our reality
Yet you dare to ask this of me?

Shall I lean over and allow a ladder to uncurl from my mind

To guide you into this reality of mine
Where my enemies and friends reside
And from your treatment hide?

I fight through my medication withdrawal, and my friends try their best to distract me: we have a picnic and paint each other's fingernails and horns.

As the sun sets, a dusty, muggy fog looms. I get lost in my attempt to feign control. I overanalyze and dizzy myself. I can't find what I'm looking for, and my friends are replaced by laughing stains of cruel energies. They criticize so loudly, and their assumptions are strangling. I want to slip away, be free from them, but I cannot find any blades. Anything with an edge, perhaps a shard from a mirror... The stains click their tongues, judging my desires.

"Oh, Self Injury"

I am evil for wanting to do as I please, yet you're not evil for wanting to control me? This is my life, whose end I should decide on my own. I don't care if my chosen exit is not something you condone. 'But that's so selfish! They'll be sad!' Oh, yes, but what you do is not? Keeping someone around who only wants for life to stop? Every day is a chore. Every word spoken is shit. I'm just an angry annoyance. As if I'd really be missed. Sure, people may cry, 'it just wasn't her time. She ought to have stayed alive. Surely she didn't really long to die!' It really is amusing that you think you know what's in my head, yet you ignore or dismiss what emotional words I have said.

Well, so be it! I'll let you assume I have 'no good reasons' behind how I feel. That I was just confused, overreacting, simply in need of some help. Well, help me! Help me! Strap me down and observe. Take away my blades— that will certainly preserve this skin, now scared, from my reckless abuse, because, after, many many years, this pattern should easily come loose. I do feel, so deeply, yet prefer not to shout. I'd rather keep it to myself, rather bleed my tears out. You'd prefer I'm wailing, arguing? That I smoke a cigarette? Have a drink? There are many types of recreation and coping; I'll do what works best for me. Yes, I must do this for attention. Look at me! Look at me! That's why I hide in my room where no one can see. I'm already aware of my addiction, so I don't need you to confirm. If anything, I'd ask that you take time to shut up, pay attention, and learn: these marks are not made to kill me, but to pull me away from the whispers and temptations that I fight every day. Slap a label on my forehead, or tell me that I am wrong. That I'm a dramatic nutcase whose pleasures are too sick to calm, who needs to just get over herself and learn to be strong. Because my intention is obviously to be coddled, apparently it has been all along! Unfortunately for you, I don't abide by how others think. I have my own voice and will decide how best I speak. The whispers are the enemies. The cuts are my friends who pull me away from danger, who keep me from my end.

For as I drug myself to sleep, I close my eyes and hope to keep those prying
monsters in my mind who lift me, laughing, as I cry. I do not fear the monsters,
no, nor where they take me as I float. Through halls and tunnels adorned with
fear, beautiful faces smiling as I fly near. A clock tick tocks inside my chest. My
body pulsates with each breath. I sweat, I shiver, I grind my teeth as voices
whisper from both above and beneath: 'We'll help you down and up' they sing
with glee. 'We'll destroy those monsters, set you free.' How wonderful I
sometimes think it'd be to let those voices comfort me. But the monsters are too
strong for them, and the voices do fade in the end. And when I am dropped
down back onto my bed and feel remnants of the night's dread, I wish to sink,
down, down into the ground— to smile, gratefully, as I drown. For every day is a
struggle to survive as I carry on with my painted life.

More voices mock, "Oh, Golly Gee, it's a sad Emily!" They laugh
and I try to tell them to leave, but I can't speak. Everything around me
dissolves and I'm surrounded by mirrors. Images dance out from them,
masquerading as friends, as my fellow Trickies, preying upon my open
heart. I hear overlapping eulogies for my selves while gleeful voices sing:

"They's a Gonner"

Oh, golly gee
What a mess there'll be
Gotta stain they gotta clean
From a dead Emily

Oh my golly gosh
They's a gonner
And the body's gettin' smelly— ain't it rough?
Oh my golly gosh
They's a gonner
And they gonna call the flies
So clean 'Em up

There's blood pooling beneath me. It's sticky and smells like
solitary nights spent cleaning up self-inflicted wounds. If I try to get up, I
slip and the bloody pool deepens. I let it fill only a few inches before
resigning myself and lying down on my back. I don't want to look at the
mirrors. On the ceiling are projected memories of unkind forms; they lull
me into a daydream.

"Knots"

Flies in our tea and knots in our stomach
Hot glued fingers and gems in the pocket
Sip and glue, set, place, and sigh
Bedazzled skulls don't want to die

Incense ash makes home of the carpet
Hills on the desk, slide our fingers, define it
Watered down but we mustn't waste
Dip your fingers; press that ash to paste

"Worm"

Inside out or outside in
Let him, please, sometime crawl in
He needs food— you're quite the bite
So won't you let him feast tonight?
Kind and soft
Teeth so long
Will always thank you with a song

He wiggles down your throat so tight
To find some meat that smells just right
He's fond of muscle— slurps up lard
His favorite: tender, pulsing hearts
Kind and soft
Teeth so long
Will always thank you with a song

Inside out or outside in
Let me please, sometime crawl in
I need food— you're quite the bite
So won't you let me feast tonight?
I'm kind and soft
My teeth are long
And nibble, nibble, slowly, 'til you're all gone!

"Plaything"

Shuffle on home, boy. Fast as you can, boy.
Play with your toy, boy. Feed your beast.
It's all alone, boy. While you have fun, boy.
Think how it feels, boy. Where it can't see.
Wet and moldy, cold and sad
—To hear the laughter and fire crack
Eyes that stopped working, too long in the dark
Oh!
I'd give my life for one night in the park

Blood is in my throat, coagulating and choking me. I can't call out. How will anyone know how to find me? Who still likes me enough to help? I've pushed so many away. My body begins to sink. Perhaps I deserve to drown.

I hear a voice and feel a soft pull on my heart– a reminder. My Love, the Mountain Man, pulls me out of my self-sabotage. He reminds me of my friends. Of music and art and joy. Of possibilities. His dogs lick my face. I open my eyes. The projections are gone. The blood I lie in is absorbed back into the Earth. My throat is clear. The mirrors disappear. I'm back in the woods.

My wounds close and rays of sunlight peek through the trees and make my scars glitter.

My Love helps me up and we hug tightly; our energies merge and we are both comforted.

"Sometimes"

I recognize your energy
A swirling, cosmic memory
Manifesting near to me
I know you're always dear

Delicate, pulsing, pulling dream
A warming, guiding melody
Invoking vibrating harmonies
Which help me to remember

Sometimes– I am your lover
And sometimes– we hardly know one another
But I find you in my gaze
Always, always
Sometimes– I stand tall with my antlers
And sometimes– I fly with my feathers
I find I've all forms, many tethers
Met all Earthly ends– love, death, decay I defend

Skipping, joyful, full of glee
On the hillside next to me
Warming in the mellow breeze
–a glimpse of recognition

Coaxing the campfire's charming core
Puts us at ease so our hearts can soar
To each potential we explore
I can tell by the moments which linger

Sometimes– I am your lover
And sometimes– we hardly know one another
But I find you in my gaze
Always, always
Sometimes– I swim fast with my flippers

And sometimes— I build dams by the river
I find in my eyes your soul glimmers
Know you before every end— love, death, decay I defend

My light shines in and out of time
And I try to recognize in every life
In the hope that my spirit comes through
And that it leads me to you

I glide in and out of time
Adventure through every life
In the hope that my spirit comes through
And that it leads me to you, sometimes

My Tricky friends and the elementals are not visible, but I can feel them.

My Love and his dogs walk with me to his cabin. We sit on a bench on his porch. His dogs lay down and fall asleep. The night is cool and cleansing.

We sit in a comfortable silence, leaning on one another. I begin to drift into a most blissful sleep. My energy leaves my sleeping form, content to leave that version with her love in the woods.

A fox spirit manifests and I follow it deep into the woods, deeper than I've ever been before. I follow it to a birch tree that is wrapped in a spiral stairway.

As we climb it, the fox speaks aloud my thoughts, "Never be ashamed to love. It makes you stronger. Yes, it's important to find strength in solitude, to be sure of yourself, but it's also important to be able to let yourself be loved, and to trust in that love. Remember, the brighter your love, the more easy it is to find. We support each other with our love, dancing through the cosmos, rejoining to comfort and support each other every time we wake up."

The stairs go beyond the top of the tree. They extend out of the atmosphere, past planets and stars, before ending abruptly.

It's dark here. Beautiful.

The fox spirit points to the edge with its nose. "Death will guide you the rest of the way."

"I know. Thanks. I'm sorry I don't remember you very well. But I know we were friends once."

"Many times."

I close my eyes and try to remember my friend. After a few moments, I say, "I found you once. I was a human and you had been skinned alive. You wandered into my garage. You found me and you died and I held you and mourned you and buried you in the woods."

"Yes. My name is Varney. You guided me to Death at that time, and so I do the same for you when I can."

I hug Varney and then step off of the staircase. Instead of empty space, I find myself walking on familiar green carpet through a narrow corridor. Colorful art pieces line the hallway. I hear Death's hum surround me as I admire the creations; I feel such pride in them.

A spider-like insect flies past me, redirecting my attention. I can see chapel doors at the end of the hall. The closer I get, the wider the hallway becomes.

Before I reach the doors, Death manifests in front of me. I stop, gazing up at the marvelous energy. We are silent as we look at each other, and I dip into a slight bow. Death does the same and says, "You are loved, Hermit."

I am overwhelmed with memories of joy. I give Death a long hug as it explains, "You left your 'Garden Party' invitation at your Love's cabin. I brought it back for you." I step back and take the envelope. I don't open it right away, but instead bow once more to Death.

"Oh, Lady Death"

Oh, Lady Death
I love you so
You guide this Hermit
To what they may know
Fun, playful, charming
Heartbreaking, severe
My darling, so dear
Of warmth, of revere— my heart feels you near
Oh, Lady Death,
(Oh, Love)

Death gently instructs, "Call upon all your guides. Don't be shy with them. And, Hermit, don't forget your heart, post-decay."

I look at my invitation. This time it reads, "You are invited to join Magickal Morose and friends for a charming afternoon in the garden. Call upon your guides and spirit to help reach the chapel doors. P.S. No need to RSVP."

"Personal Angels"

Angels, personal angels, please be mine
Guide and direct me; hold me throughout time
I'm just a fool who craves the love in you

Angels, personal angels, I feel you near
Between left, between right— as a medium I do appear
Bridging our words to find the truth in you (oh, oh what should this Hermit do?)

My guides appear as Death erupts up into the ceiling.

Death departs and I remember who I am. I remember the Hermit.

Ancestors, family, friends, lovers– those who are always a thought away– gather around me. The flying spider appears again; it takes a human-like form and joins them. They're another version of me, I think. They seem to know what I'm thinking. "*You* are a version of *me*, more like," they remark. "You're like a pinky off on its own journey."

"A pinky," I repeat flatly.

"A very important pinky!"

"Are you also called 'Emily'?"

"You can call me that, but I like to call myself Magickal Morose."

"That's dramatic."

Magickal Morose smiles. "I know. I enjoy it." They pick up on my flickering doubt and ask, "what *if* it's all in your head?"

I think before finally giving my answer: "It really doesn't matter. My favored 'delusions' are more beautiful than they are destructive. They have helped me to not be cruel to myself.

"I am a Death Witch. I honor and walk with Death– gladly, freely, with love. I am better for it.

"We find representations of our own dualities; mine is in the dark. In the chaos. We attract elements potentially dangerous, detestable, but we find something to love and admire within such would-be faults. This is important– learning to identify the shadow, accept it, understand it, and to find a love to cherish in it.

It's not about what we deserve, but what we've learned and how we've reflected.

I spent far too long fighting my empathy."

"A Promising Shadow"

Both the left and right ignite
More the below to the above– though we share similar sights
Working in tandem so love in the universe can grow
Consistently yearn to experience, to know

We remember who we are
Find confidence, address our faults, our woes
As we revisit the peace of our stellar cribs
Our spirit blossoms, an astral rose

"I am looking for what so many spend their lives trying to avoid. Fear of it fuels the actions of many. For me, instead of fear, there is curiosity. Thrill. Enlightenment. Or is it that I don't correlate fear with negativity? Fear can be beneficial as caution– part of learning is being at first uncomfortable, surely. But I find the heart in Death: it is what creates and encourages a heart's value. And so I spend dreams seeking out that which others often cite as an evil.

"I can feel too much– an overactive amygdala whose dramatics switch on or off; I'm either all or nothing. A nice personality disorder to accompany my sentient flesh. The three-dimensional way of experiencing time feels slow and heavy. In my sleep, my dreams, I move so quickly. Time is nothing, and I can jump through cracks and through corners and into nooks, into faucets and mirrors and walls. My spirit is not limited, and I remember more of myself. I visit regular moments, shops and homes, different variations of myself and my paths, and hope I continue to retain the information I recover in my sleep when I am flesh.

"As a Death Witch and a Hermit, I work with Death, in my own way, for I have a love for Death and a promise to myself to do what I can to honor it. I always have a connection to the dead and dying and to those grieving the dead and dying, and I wish to continue to enhance and share my skills. One of my bodies died. My spirit collected itself. It's always in a cycle of recollecting itself. I feel Death like a spider feels a tug on its web. I am an epilogue to many, a prologue to some, with love for all.

"There is strength and necessity for the novel and unfamiliar. I am a collection of energies meant to listen, learn, protect, and guide. I must learn patience before fury as well as patience within fury. I love to haunt, and I accept being an Oracle of Death. Existing in between. Sharing sorrows." And I'm still curious. "Magickal Morose?"

"Yes?"

"Did we make the Treehouse?"

"Yes."

"So, I can go back? I think I want to stay there and help spirits."

"That's why we made it. You run it."

"I thought Jodi was in charge..."

"Oh, Jodi's an employee. They're the branch manager and I couldn't flourish without them, but you're the director there."

"That sounds like a lot of responsibility."

"It is. You can do it."

"I know."

"The Hermit's Lesson (The Lament's Echo)"

To meet those I walk with at night, sharing my bright light
A torch, a guide– all welcome here in my eyes (gathering, gathering)
All forms of spirits arrive
Your energies, equal, feel grace, feel freedom
As pains no longer emerge– absorbed, washed, burned
Now it's respite, so warm, so secure

Speak– I may hear it
In this Treehouse for the Spirits
This Hermit's purpose is to listen and to learn

And if spirits are lost, they can look for my lights that will lead them to the Treehouse.

"My Goblin Lights"

My Goblin Lights
So murky, soggy, bright
Pink and yellow guides

My invitation turns into pink and yellow lights that float up, popping like bubbles as they reach the ceiling.

I knock on the chapel doors. My Love answers the door and Magickal Morose careens into him and gives him a kiss. He smiles at us both.

All my loved ones roam the garden. Many versions of myself are here as well: different variations of the same heart.

Emily's Garden

We create our own devils. Perhaps you'd dance with mine, or perhaps I'd dance with yours. Maybe they'd dance with each other while we dance.

It's okay to have been wrong. It's okay to need to improve. Life, existence, is learning. Lessons. To eventually remember ourselves.

Death is not evil. Death guides, caresses, encompasses. Grief tugs and tears and turns us bitter against it. But Death is neutral. Ambivalent; objective; playful; creative; merciful; severe; abrasive; gentle; affirming. It is intense. Severe, mesmerizing– I swoon over it. I honor it; it encourages the heart within my memories.

Magickal Morose's Treehouse

It's a rule of the Treehouse that it is a place of respite. You must leave your ill wills at the door. Any are welcome, and, as we are all Travelers here, no one is better than the other, no matter what forms we have or have not taken. A place of refuge. To recharge. To rest. To reside. A hotel. A home.

Stay true to who you are fresh from the stars.

About the Author:

Emily Carol is a wannabe cryptid from Fresno, CA. They currently live in a coastal Californian town with their partner and three cats. They enjoy playing the cello, hiking, swimming, talking to ghosts, and painting.